In affection.

Julianne Royston

GW00721711

THE PENHALE HEIRESS

This is the story of four women and their love for the same man – Robert Fursdon.

Lady Eleanor, his pale, plain, aristocratic wife whom he married for status; the pretty Felicity who is transformed into a fearful old witch; Elizabeth, tempestuous and beautiful; and finally her mother, Margaret Penhale, mistress of High Coombe.

Their passions lead to their own destructions in this fascinating tale of the great house of High Coombe, the Penhale heritage, set against the backcloth of Elizabethan England, the intrigues of its court, the adventures of its sailors and the initiatives of the new breed of merchants and entrepreneurs like Robert Fursdon himself.

Julianne Royston has a sequel, *The Penhale Fortune*, in preparation. This tells the story of Robert's two children, Penelope Penhale Fursdon and Carew Gray, introduced in this the first book of the saga.

THE PENHALE HEIRESS

JULIANNE ROYSTON

ROBERT HALE · LONDON

© Julianne Royston 1988
First published in Great Britain 1988

ISBN 0 7090 3463 6

Robert Hale Limited
Clerkenwell House
Clerkenwell Green
London EC1R 0HT

Photoset in North Wales by
Derek Doyle & Associates, Mold, Clwyd.
Printed in Great Britain by
WBC Print Ltd., Barton Manor, Bristol.
Bound by WBC Bookbinders Limited.

To my parents
in love and gratitude

'Oh what a tangled web we weave,
When first we practise to deceive!'

Sir Walter Scott

PART ONE 1572–1577
Nicholas

1 Arrivals

As Nicholas Trenow rode up through the Exe valley towards his home in east Devon, the early morning mist still clung in sparkling droplets to the fresh green leaves overhead. For here and there the sun was breaking through in a glory of brilliant light, illuminating the lush woodland and its magnificent underground haze of bluebells. The may trees were in full bloom and recalled, for Nicholas, earlier Maydays when he had lain with local girls in the meadows of his stepfather's farm.

How long ago it all seemed, another world, for since then Nicholas had voyaged with Drake halfway round the world, had shivered in damp clothes below decks, so close-bound beneath leaking timbers that he felt that he was already in his grave. By contrast, journeying across land in search of gold, the searing sun bore down upon him till every drop of moisture seemed drawn out of his body, leaving a bone-weariness. He remembered storms at sea, so violent that the little ship seemed certain never to ride up from the trough above the towering twenty-foot waves.

Nicholas surveyed the peace of his beloved county and heard the early morning chorus of blackbird, thrush and tit. As he left the Exe, he had seen the herons rise strong-winged over the grey waters of the river. He did not miss the quarrelsome and repetitive argument of the seagulls left behind. He urged his tired mare up the steep woodland paths, anxious to be on the land of his stepfather, John Vigus.

Nicholas remembered John in anger and pain, anger because he had hated the thought of his aristocratic mother's marriage to this plain countryman and pain that he had always rejected John's amiable advances towards him. Eventually his stepfather had ceased to try and had given all his love to a brood of young Viguses, especially Nicholas' eldest stepsister, Felicity. This stepsister was made in the image of her beautiful mother, thick fair tresses which were always untidy and fell about a sensual face, with creamy skin, wide generous mouth and green eyes.

Nicholas always saw his mother as a young woman, although the lovely girl was worn out with heavy farm duties and frequent childbearing; she had become a fat slattern whose beautiful face had become marred with a perpetual expression of resentment and anger. Her son might have recalled the frequent beatings at his mother's hands of her fury that elopement in a state of advanced pregnancy with the handsome groom, Adam Trenow, had led to her banishment from the family estates of the wealthy and aristocratic Carews. Over the years, Elizabeth had worked out all her disappointments on the child of this marriage, Nicholas. For, a month after her wedding, her groom had fallen ill and died. But for the kindness of John Vigus, who had plucked Elizabeth and her baby from a ditch one dark night, both would have perished.

Above all things, Nicholas desired to present himself to his mother, to throw at her feet the gold pieces earned from his last long and dangerous voyage to the Americas; he longed to say to her, 'Now you may enter into your heritage. You may have servants, rich clothing, a gaily accoutred mount to ride out on to visit your neighbours.' In his mind's eye, he saw Elizabeth, dressed out once more as the fine lady, he saw her embracing him with a warmth that she had never shown before. So, as he rode up the narrow lane to the farmhouse, early as it was, he expected to see her standing, as she so often did, at the farmhouse door, shielding her eyes from the sun and gazing down across the valley towards Cornwall and her long lost childhood home. As always, the farmyard was deep in mire; the cattle were lowing from their stalls, ready for milking, the dogs, shut away in the barn, barked shrilly, hearing a stranger, not the long-lost son of the house, a house which still lay silent in the slumber of its inhabitants. The uneven thatch, moss-covered in places, the broken shutters, revealed poverty and neglect, offset by the sturdiness of the thick wattle and daub walls and the fine timbers, where house and barn merged in a solid whole. It all seemed so much smaller to Nicholas than on that day when he had run away to sea to seek his fortune, impatient with the local rector who was his tutor and frustrated by the constant tormenting of the village boys, who respected him for his physical prowess, but resented this education, which set him aside, even from his half-brothers.

Nicholas shrugged it all off as he dismounted and led his weary mount into the stables, where, despite his impatience, he took time to unsaddle her and present her with a generous ration of oats. Still no-one stirred in the slumbering house and, entering through the side door, Nicholas stumbled over the sleeping bodies of farm-servants in the gloom of the shuttered kitchen, illuminated by the embers of the dying fire in the great chimney-piece. Ignoring the mutterings and grunts of the newly awakened men, he made his way up the narrow stairs to the rooms above, where the family now slept. John Vigus had flourished sufficiently to add a storey to his small farmhouse, in deference to his lady wife.

Nicholas burst into her bedchamber and threw open the coarse bed-curtains, to behold the startled features of John Vigus and a young girl whom he had never seen before. 'Why you whoreson,' he said. 'Where is she? What have you done with her.'

In his sleepy state, John hardly recognised his stepson. The gangling boy was now a sturdy thickset man with a wild reddish beard under beetling brows. 'Nick, is it you, lad? Hold your horses' – and then, as Nicholas dragged him from the bed, 'Nick, your mother is dead, two years past.'

His stepson released his grasp, unceremoniously dropping the old man back on the mattress, and stared. In a low voice, 'It's not true. Please God I'll forgive you, if you will just say that it is a story, no more than an excuse for this.' He pointed at the lass in his stepfather's bed, a young girl, now snivelling in fright at the sudden appearance of this stranger.

'Would to God it were not. But she's gone, lad, and no word from you.'

Nicholas stumbled back through the now awakened household where the labourers stood awkwardly rubbing the sleep out of their eyes and hastily lacing their breeches. One found presence of mind to throw back the shutters, revealing the confusion of a household thrown out of its usual slow routine. The sunlight was dazzling, seeming to deaden the fire completely, and showing the farmhouse up in its smoke-darkened interior. The floor was filthy, although strewn with rushes, and the crude furniture was encrusted with long-forgotten meals, pork fat and oatmeal.

In his grief the stricken young man saw none of this, but retraced his footsteps down the lane. He ran blindly on and on, the thorns of overhanging branches scratching his face and the fallen trunks and great boulders bruising his knees and ankles, as he stumbled on with one thought on his mind. Now she would never love him. She would never recognise that he wanted to repay her for the agony of her lost youth and wasted life. He had lost the opportunity to tell her that he did not care about the beatings if only she would forgive him for being alive. He flung himself down into the rich soil of decaying leaves. As he sobbed, he became aware of myriads of insects going about their business, ants carrying immense loads, centipedes and a beetle or two; every now and then one flew off into the sun. At the level of his eyes he watched, bemused, whilst the tears dried on his cheeks. He sat up, clasping his knees to him. Grief had drained him dry; he could no longer think or feel anything.

So Felicity found him hours later, and the dogs, gambolling about her feet, barked when they discovered the silent stranger sitting at the foot of an immense beech tree. Nicholas looked up sharply. 'Jasper,' he called. Suddenly the tears returned, for Jasper too must be long dead in the years between. He had locked him in the barn as he left, hearing the dog's cries as he ran off towards Plymouth and the sea. So strong was the bond of understanding between brother and sister that Felicity immediately sensed what was in his mind, 'Jasper died of old age last year, but this is his daughter, Jess.' Sure enough a small ball of fluff, hardly distinguishable as a spaniel, since her mother was a nondescript farm bitch, launched herself at him, giving his nose a sharp nip. To his surprise, Nicholas laughed.

Over the weeks that followed, the pain gave way to anger, anger now directed against all women for their treachery. John was kindness itself; his half-brothers were indifferent but not hostile. Village cronies were agog to hear of his adventures, for Drake's fame was known throughout the West Country. John Vigus refused to accept any of the small hoard of gold which Nicholas brought with him, but advised his stepson to seek his fortune up-country. Nicholas was no farmer; anyway the smallholding would provide no more than a bare living for John's own eldest son. For the first time Nicholas recognised John's generosity and kindness over the years. He promised his stepfather and Felicity that he would return and Felicity shyly introduced him to her swain, Tom Gray, an older man who tilled a neighbouring farm.

When Nicholas saddled his mare, now skittish from lack of exercise, and called Jess to him, for she was firmly his dog and scorned farm duties for the carefree strolls and country walks with a new master, he turned in the saddle to look his stepfather in the eye, and thanked him for everything. It was Felicity's turn to weep. 'Come on, sis, I have a mind to find an heiress. When I have, you shall come a'visiting and play the great lady. I know you have a mind to it.' The ridicule in his voice made her look up sharply. How had Nicholas known? Then she and her father exchanged knowing glances, for Nicholas had an eye to the women, always had, and they flocked for his attention, even in the few short weeks he had been home. The thought in both their minds was that Nicholas would surely snare some innocent young maid.

Old John had a sense of humour and laughed when Nicholas rode off, an excited Jess at his heels. 'The bitches will always follow him, eh lass?' Felicity turned away, aware of disappointment now that Nicholas' exciting and unpredictable presence was removed. Poor dear faithful Tom Gray seemed so boring, but he was all she had or was likely to have.

* * *

Margaret Penhale could not be described as either pretty or beautiful. But her air of good health, allied to that of innocence, produced an effect upon the onlooker. She had a cloud of chestnut hair which was always escaping from her caps and framing her oval face in a mass of unruly curls. Her deep brown eyes, set wide apart, were her great beauty. Her nose and mouth were large and her complexion clear and tanned. On this particular May morning in 1572 she was full of high spirits and rode her fine grey mare over the hills high above the estuary. It was a view that she adored, combining river, sea, sky and woodland in a clear panorama. Like her great Queen, Elizabeth, Margaret loved England, which she was always to associate with this view over the Exe.

On this occasion, as she so frequently did, she had left her father some way behind and therefore rode alone and almost full pelt into a young man who was coming pensively up through the woods, a young man in his prime, eighteen years of age, short but powerfully built. Five years at sea had built up muscle, as they had also matured him, to the extent that he looked older than his years. He was deeply tanned by Caribbean sun and long months at sea. His blue eyes sparkled above a profuse ruddy beard which disguised a formidable chin. The sparkle was produced by the sight of this lovely young woman. As a young unmarried girl, her fine chestnut hair was uncovered and hung in tangled curls down her back. Her peach complexion was flushed with exertion. She wore a rather old-fashioned gown but it was made of fine imported dark green velvet. The kirtle was of a light russet and despite the low-cut décolletage the fine young figure was masked with a cream coloured embroidered chemise. The heavy full sleeves were folded back to reveal fine fox fur which matched her glorious hair. In later years Nicholas was to describe Margaret as 'bonny' rather than beautiful. But the first impression was one of beauty.

At this moment their eyes met and held. There was an instant attraction and he bowed low over the saddle. 'Madam, I appear to have lost my way and am seeking High Coombe and Sir Henry Penhale, who is acquainted with my friend Francis Drake.'

'Sir, he rides some paces behind' – at that moment her father loomed out of the brushwood, frowning impatiently.

'Margaret, must you always gallop on ahead? It is a dangerous practice.' He stopped dead in his tracks, pulling his horse up sharply, on sight of the handsome young man.

'Nicholas Carew Trenow at your service, sir. Francis Drake commends me to you and sends messages of goodwill.'

'Indeed, I believed him to be overseas.'

'He is returning shortly. We have had a fair voyage and some success in our attack on the Spaniards.' Even Nicholas was not fully aware of the triumph which Drake was to make out of an early attack on the Isthmus of Darien, as the ship on which Nicholas had been travelling had returned early. Nicholas was hardly known to Drake, but with typical boldness he used his acquaintance to introduce himself to the Penhales.

The Penhales, like the Drakes and the Hawkins, were of modest origin, far more so than the Carews. However, shrewd exploitation of a commissioner's position at the time of King Henry's break with Rome and the dissolution of the monasteries had brought the abbey into the hands of Sir Henry.

Wall by wall, the abbey had been dismantled and the stone had been carried down to an opening in the Foxhole Gap in the local hills where a commanding position gave the new house, High Coombe, a glimpse of the sea beyond. It stood solid on the hillside; on this particular day of Nicholas' arrival, the glass of the fine and expensive windows winked in the bright sun. Inside, these same high mullions gave a light and airy aspect to the Great Hall. The corner of the east wing fronted on to an elaborate terrace and ornamented garden and here was the solar, so called by the old-fashioned Sir Henry, who secretly would have been quite content with one great room to serve all purposes. But his gentle wife, long since dead, had insisted on this room with its moulded ceiling, painted in brighter colours and elaborately gilded. The estate's fine oaks had provided linen-fold panelling of high quality in hall and parlour alike. In the west wing were servants' quarters and a great kitchen serving a multitude of retainers and labourers. Above the hall a minstrels' gallery ran from east to west and enabled Sir Henry's daughter to listen in to the conversation of her elders in the hall below. From hence she could slip away down a handsome staircase to her own bedchamber and those of her guests sited along the corridor in the east wing. Above these rooms was a long gallery of some sixty-five feet, floored in solid oak and adorned with portraits of past Penhales, painted from memory by a local artist.

Nicholas was suitably impressed as his host welcomed him at the door, dispatching a servant with his horse and dog round the great mass of stables and barns at the back of the house. Escorted to his bedchamber, he found a room adorned with the finest tapestries and a great four-poster, hung with embroidered curtains. A man-servant unpacked his few belongings into a large chest at the foot of the bed and Nicholas was guided back to the Great Hall where a meal of a piece of boiled beef, a baked leg of mutton, two coneys, a neat's tongue and two warden pies was set before him. To beer, was also added some delicious sweet French wine from Bordeaux. His host informed him that one of the Penhales' activities was the import of wine from both the Rhenish and French vineyards. Retiring that evening to the long gallery, Margaret played upon the virginals and Nicholas was given the viol at his request; two servants played upon the lute and the gittern. The latter was an instrument which Nicholas had not seen before. It had a long neck, rounded back and oval-shaped body. It provided an excellent accompaniment to the soft sweet voice of his hostess.

From his comfortable bed, Nicholas contemplated the opportunities. Here was a charming heiress of pleasing countenance, an excellent bosom and neat ankles. He had glimpsed the latter as she dismounted upon her arrival back at High Coombe. She was obviously a competent housekeeper, the keys jingled from her waist, her servants went happily about their work. The lad who had attended Nicholas in his bedchamber chatted easily of his master and mistress and their standing in the countryside. Their wealth was obvious on every side. On his way down to High Coombe, Sir Henry had pointed out to him flocks of the finest sheep and a range of magnificent horses grazing in the lower paddock. Immediately here was a subject of common interest, for despite his time at sea, Nicholas had not forgotten or lost his interest in the schooling of horses of all kinds. So he drifted into sleep, down a vision of a blissful future with a lovely heiress and a fine fortune.

It was therefore something of a shock to rise the next morning to another sunny day and a descent to the parlour, to be greeted by an elderly man, stooped and grey, who was introduced as Margaret's neighbour and future husband, Sir Richard Bourne. He was obviously a man of wealth and standing. His clothes were old-fashioned to Nicholas' eye, but of the finest woollen cloth. His horse's accoutrements were of the very best leather and adorned with silver. Nicholas noted this, as he watched Margaret and her betrothed trot out of the stable-yard and towards Bourne, to the west of High Coombe.

Sir Henry was courteous but cool. He invited Nicholas to join him on a visit to an outlying farm. The tenant had complained about his leaking roof and the condition of his barns: Sir Henry's farm bailiff had assured him that all was well and recommended that a new tenant be found next Lady Day. Sir Henry wanted to investigate for himself. So he and his guest rode north out across the estate taking the coastal route. The sea was calm, the very smallest of wavelets rippling and sparkling in the sunshine. Nicholas began to tell of an adventure in mid-Atlantic when his ship lay becalmed for over a week. The sailors, including Nicholas, had to get out a row-boat and attempt to tow the ship into a wind. It was very hot and dry and some of the men fainted. Nicholas' endurance on that occasion endeared him to the captain and thus began Nicholas' promotion to trusty lieutenant. 'So many of my shipmates died that anyone who survived was bound to get more of the booty,' commented Nicholas, modestly. With cunning, he was giving the impression that he had more wealth than the few gold coins which he had in his possession. For Nicholas knew that Sir Henry was inspecting him, curious about this young man who had ridden in out of the blue. Sir Henry was aware, as was the whole county, of the Carew scandal, but the offspring was an unknown quantity to the local gentry. Sir Henry was surprised that he was so well-educated in matters of intellect, as well as culture. The musical talent was entirely unexpected. His interest in the hawks and hunting was perhaps less so, as tenant farmers pursued this where they could. Nicholas' adventures at sea were of genuine interest and the morning went well.

In the weeks that followed, Sir Henry grew alarmed. He was courteous to travellers, but concerned that Nicholas stayed so long. He was aware of well-chaperoned riding trips that Nicholas and Margaret took into the surrounding countryside and to friends and neighbours. Sir Richard Bourne frequently accompanied them and one day broached the subject of Nicholas to Sir Henry.

Slowly, he replied to his friend's query. 'Yes, I am aware of this burgeoning friendship. But I know my daughter. Beneath that quiet exterior lurks a strong will. Oppose Margaret and you produce a reaction. But she is both sensible and responsible. I will find a means of persuading the young man to leave. He is very ambitious and I will procure him an introduction to Court.'

Sir Richard and Sir Henry were contemporaries and good friends, respecting each other, and no more was said.

Sir Henry was right in his assessment of his daughter. Margaret was increasingly drawn to her handsome young companion, and yet, at the same time, she drew back, in honour, as the affianced bride of Sir Richard Bourne. She and Nicholas rode out almost daily in the company of a groom. she talked of her motherless childhood and the solicitous care of a devoted father. She spoke, in loving terms, of the tenants: she knew them all by name and the details of their families, births, deaths, marriages, their flocks, their good and bad harvests. She knew the estate charcoal-burner, the blacksmith, the wheelwright, the turners and the joiners. Each piece of fine furniture in the house had been made locally at the request of Sir Henry or his daughter. She was particularly interested in the quality of different kinds of timber. Here Nicholas would talk about shipbuilding and the local sources for Topsham yards. Invariably their conversation turned to horses and the Arab strain of the High Coombe stock. On several occasions Nicholas was allowed to join her in the schooling of a particular stallion. They rejoiced together at the birth of two foals, crouching together over the labours of a mare in a difficult and protracted birth. By contrast, they sauntered through the woods in the sleepy warmth of a summer day, leaving the groom in attendance on their horses. It seemed natural and inevitable that Margaret was drawn into Nicholas' arms for a long, lingering kiss. He gentled her as he would a restive foal, stroking her cheeks and tickling her nose with a straw. 'You know I must marry Sir Richard, who is so good to me.'

'Of course, sweetheart, but it does not prevent me from loving you.' Thus it was out and she drew back; to him, more like a startled fawn than ever.

'Please, please say no more. I can never accompany you again if you do.'

"Tis my last declaration.' Here Nicholas went on one knee, playing the fool and laughing. But his eyes were serious. 'Come with me and be my love.'

Margaret reached out and stroked the russet head and ran pell-mell up the path to where the groom waited.

Next day they were off again, this time to visit an old lady, whom Margaret had befriended. She lived in a remote hamlet in a tiny cottage, so Nicholas lingered at the door whilst Margaret carried eggs and butter into a darkened interior. As they rode away, Margaret said, 'I wonder what will happen to me if I live long years.' She turned in the saddle and found herself gazing into Nicholas' eyes, which were full of love and longing. The groom dallied behind so they set their horses to a canter, pulling up on the brow of the hill. The horses were winded and they dismounted, withdrawing once more into a woodland glade. As Margaret settled upon the grass she knew the danger, but she longed to hear Nicholas speak once more of his love. She knew that he must depart soon; already her father had spoken of securing him some patronage at Court. But now Nicholas was beside her, bending over and gently pulling her hair. 'Untidy girl, you can never keep it under control.' And his arm was about her shoulder and his other hand under her chin. It was a lingering kiss, her lips opened to his and her mouth was warm and sweet. Her eyes were wide, gazing into his. It was as though he drew her into his own and he sighed,

'Nicholas. Oh, Nicholas. It can never be.' To his fury, Nicholas found that Jess launched herself into Margaret's lap. The moment was broken by laughter on Margaret's part; she drew away, shaking her skirt, standing up and walking demurely down the track, eyes downcast. As he caught her up, she disengaged his arm. 'Careful, my love. Will is only just round that corner.'

In early September, just as the leaves were beginning to change colour and the bright hot days of August were behind, Nicholas and Margaret rode with the groom to try out a new bird. Nicholas had not revealed his limited experience of falconry but, typically, had learnt quickly from the Penhales' falconer and practised hard when the Penhales were elsewhere. The servants were very curious about this young man, who dressed well and spoke well, but who obviously had no fortune. The young mistress was well-loved and the servants did not miss the loving glances and affectionate banter of the young couple. Will, the groom, wanted to meet a young maid from his native village and he contrived to let Margaret know, so that, on this particular morning, he was released to ride off up the valley to his trysting place and Margaret and Nicholas were alone.

In the weeks since Nicholas' arrival Margaret had barely acknowledged to herself the strength of her feelings for him. But she was aware of a tremendous enthusiasm for living and a deep joy. Despite her mother's early death, Margaret had always been able to savour every moment of her happy life. Each morning she woke to new adventures. Like the great Queen, Margaret had been well-tutured in languages, theology and the classics. She had grown up strong and confident. She was aware that neighbours' sons vied for her approval, for she knew her worth in terms of lands and wealth. What she did not know was her worth as a woman. Nicholas' subtle attentions had awoken her for the first time. On this morning, the weather was heavy and the sky overcast. Unusually, Nicholas forebore any light and humorous chatter. Margaret turned in the saddle to ask him about his silence and he looked at her gravely. 'Margaret, tell me, do you love me as I love you?'

The horses paused, the air hung heavy and Margaret looked away. 'In November I shall marry Richard; I am a loyal friend and a loyal daughter.'

'Margaret, my beautiful Margaret, we are not talking of lands, estates, legal settlements, we are talking of love. You are so serene, so full of laughter, so intelligent; I give you my devotion, my heart, my life. Please walk with me.'

For one moment, Margaret felt that she must ride off fast, away back to High Coombe, to Bourne, to sanity. She knew that, once dismounted, she was lost. She felt a trembling in all her limbs, and yet at the same time a great exultation. Her heart was pounding. Nicholas put his arms round her waist, gently drawing her out of the saddle. He held her close, felt her tremble, saw her shut her eyes. He kissed her closed lids, her ears, nose and finally her mouth. They sank into the bracken. The horses grazed close by. A lone buzzard rose in the sky, its mournful cry echoing across the hills. Margaret opened her eyes. 'Nicholas, Nicholas, I shall never love anyone as I love you. Love me, love me.'

Again and again their passion rose and fell, till, spent, Margaret lay back on the golden fronds, gazing into an angry sky, with storm clouds lowering over the horizon. A deep clap of thunder followed by a flash of lightning growled, echoing round the valley. Reluctantly, Nicholas rose, dusting off his fine slashed breeches, and helping Margaret to her feet said, 'Let us make for that barn for shelter. It is going to rain hard.' Laughing and breathless, hand in hand, they raced through the long grass: a heavy downpour obscured the barn opening where they sheltered. Margaret leaned languorously and sleepily against her lover's shoulder, savouring the ecstasy of the past hour. He stayed silent, moved almost beyond endurance by the deep passion of this young girl. He had set out to seduce her: now he was unexpectedly shaken by her vulnerability. Her responses had surprised him: unlike most virgins, she had neither held back or expressed fear; she had moved to meet him in a glory and a passion that he had not met before. He was ashamed of his seduction and its motives. So that it was he who recalled them to the world outside as the rain abated. They rode back in silence to the meeting-place with Will.

As they cantered into the courtyard at High Coombe, Sir Henry appeared in the doorway. 'Nicholas, my old friend Sir John Gauldnay has arrived on his way to Court. He has volunteered to escort you and present you to the Queen.'

Nicholas was confused and he did not answer his host. It was Margaret who dismounted and went forward to greet Sir John. That night she drew Nicholas on one side, 'You must go. It is a wonderful opportunity, not to be missed.'

Her lover turned. 'I will return, darling. I shall get a new commission from the Queen; we will build a ship for the Indies: great fortunes await us there.' Margaret turned away; her face was filled with a great sadness and there were unshed tears in her eyes.

At that moment Sir Henry came over to join them, echoing Nicholas' last words.

Margaret turned away and said, 'I am very tired, father. I shall go to my chamber.' In the morning she did not appear.

Nicholas rode off in the company of Sir John, who was in a hurry to depart. Jess ran behind, barking excitedly in true spaniel fashion. Margaret heard the dog, whom she adored, and turned her face to the wall and wept copiously. Had she expected Nicholas to refuse Sir John's offer? If so, why had she not declared openly that she could not marry Sir Richard? She knew why; her father would never have permitted it. Nicholas' words sprang to mind: marriage was land, estates, legal settlements. Love was something else.

2   Recall

For Margaret, the next few weeks went by in a dream. There were the usual preparations made for winter, drying of herbs, salting down of meat, numerous activities in the brew house and fish house. On the farm, slaughtering, which she loathed, proceeded apace. Other animals, including horses, were sent to market. The selection of these beasts was another task which she disliked. Beneath her calm and ordered exterior, her heart raced with desires formerly unknown to her. Over and over again she relived the ecstatic moments in the bracken, each night she recalled Nicholas' face, feature by feature. She remembered the bold impudent look but she doubted his intention to return, despite the fact that he had sent her back a basket containing a bundle of fur – his beloved Jess. The dog was now her shadow, a constant reminder (as Nicholas had intended) of past passion. By the end of October she began to feel sick and faint; this was unusual, as she had always enjoyed rude good health. She dragged herself from bed in the morning, blaming her nausea on the languorous and erotic dreams which she enjoyed every night. Her old nurse Rachel, who had reared her from a newborn babe, eyed her askance and one evening came to her chamber late at night. 'My lamb, have you seen your course this month?'

'Why no, Rachel; I have been feeling poorly and I

believe that is why I missed ' She forbore to add – and in September too.

Rachel looked at her in pity. 'Mistress, is it that young rascal Nicholas?'

'What do you mean?' Margaret blushed slightly.

'Mistress, you are going to have a babe – or I be in my dotage if I am wrong.'

Margaret went pale, clutching the bed rugs to her. It could not be. Where was Nicholas now? Had he gone on another voyage, failing at Court and not daring to return? Would he ever come back? Her thoughts flew hither and thither, making her feel dazed and sick. Rachel had crept away. Jess lay at the foot of the bed, snoring contentedly. Margaret slept wretchedly and woke feeling worse than ever.

Next morning Sir Richard rode over, as he often did, and hesitantly broached the subject of their wedding. Observing her closely, he noted that she drew away from him and stood, disconsolate, in the window embrasure. She looked out at the scudding rain. It was obvious that she was miles away.

Richard was no fool; he was too old for that. He had loved and buried two wives and understood women. It made him sad to recognise that Margaret pined for that young man, but he was a realist. He was old, although not ugly or repellent in looks, but lean and grey like some old wolf. He respected Margaret for her sound character and common sense. She would forget and he could cosset her with a fine horse, clothes and possessions, even a trip to Court. Then he shied away from that. What if they met young Nicholas?

Then, to his surprise, Margaret turned and said, 'Can we bring the wedding date forward? I am sick of waiting and winter will be upon us.' She seemed to be shrugging off the dreams that beset her a few minutes ago and, loving her deeply, Richard was only too happy to accede.

In early December Margaret sat erect at the head of a

huge banqueting assembly in the Great Hall at High Coombe. Her hair, which was her one concession to vanity, hung, for the last time, uncovered in shining beauty down her back and was set off by a glorious gown of aquamarine brocade, the cloth brought especially from Italy by the devoted bridegroom. The oversleeves were lined with grey miniver. The bodice of a fine grey silk was heavily embroidered by the sewing women of High Coombe with conceits of summer flowers, pink, gold and russet. The high Medici collar was adorned with a magnificent jewelled pendant of pearls and amethyst, stones which glistened and reflected the shimmering brocade. The undersleeves were of the finest grey lawn. The bridegroom sat on her right, her proud father on her left. It was the consummation for him of the years of parenthood and planning. All the tenants and their wives were there. Friends and neighbours were full of congratulations on the bride's beauty and the groom's wealth. It was a classic marriage of neighbouring great estates. Margaret looked to her husband, where he sat, with a quiet contented smile on his lips. Guilt assailed her, but what could she have done? There had been no word from Nicholas.

After the usual dancing and high spirits, which Richard endured for her sake, they were bedded in the great chamber in the west wing. Jess, for one night was banished to the stables. On the tapestries, Diana the huntress came alive in the winds that blew around. With Rachel's help, a small deceit ensured that even her experienced husband suspected nothing. Taking Rachel's advice, Margaret played the fearful virgin. A few tears and all was done. Next morning the sheet, slightly stained with blood, would be carefully removed.

Richard slept content, snoring a little. This time genuine tears scalded Margaret's cheeks. She would never see her love again. It was a dream gone forever.

She must return to old ways – the sober and steady young woman immersed in domestic and estate affairs. Only sixteen, she could not yet reconcile herself to the loss of passion and excitement and yet, within the hour, she slept. Diana stirred on the wall, her arrow lost in the woods.

* * *

Nicholas found that his patron rode hard. As a parting gift, the Penhales had presented their guest with a splendid black stallion so that the horse at least kept pace with his companion. Nicholas' mind was elsewhere. Had he made the right decision? Yet he was sure that Margaret was his. Excluding but one, Nicholas was always to find that his women were totally caught in the mesh of his charm and fine physique. Margaret would be no exception. By the time London was reached, he had convinced himself that all would be very well indeed.

The presentation to the Queen was a great disappointment. From earliest childhood Nicholas could remember Elizabeth and John Vigus praising that young girl, who had outwitted her Catholic sister and all her enemies to mount the throne in 1558, when Nicholas was only four years old. To her distant Devonian subjects the young Queen was a dazzling goddess, who had brought England safe from the fires of Smithfield. During Nicholas' boyhood the Queen had stood firm against her enemies, in Scotland, in France and above all in Spain. The hatred of the Spanish king and his haughty courtiers ran deep and all good Englishmen blamed him for the loss of Calais and the depredations of the English Catholics. When at fourteen years of age Nicholas went to sea, he had been fired by the desire to prove himself to his mother but also by a firm ambition to serve the Virgin Queen.

Now Nicholas met her face to face; she looked magnificent, glittering with jewels. Her red wig was splayed to set off the alabaster skin and the brilliant green eyes, shrewd eyes which swept over the courtiers in all their finery, Nicholas not excepted. For his burly figure was set off to perfection in a relatively simple costume consisting of dark brown doublet and hose, slashed with orange and gold. Nicholas deeply desired some sign from the monarch that she had noticed him and had recognised the fervent passion and devotion in his eyes. Her failure to do so merely fuelled the fires of patriotism and ambition.

Nicholas was ever one to be motivated by a woman's challenge and the Queen presented one. He hung around his lodgings for two days and just as he was preparing to return to Devon, received a message to present himself at the house of Francis Walsingham. Already he was aware of Walsingham's importance – his role in guarding the Queen against her religious enemies, especially the Marian party.

When he found himself bowing to the Secretary of State, he was more than aware of the saturnine glance and the probing questions. Sir Francis trusted no-one. However, Nicholas came away with the impression that there was the prospect of employment in the future; the spymaster seemed impressed with Nicholas' grasp of affairs and surprised by his knowledge of French and Spanish, acquired from his old tutor. But Nicholas could not live on promises, so with misgivings he decided that he would go down to the shipyards on the Thames. He would then consider whether or not to take his chances once again at High Coombe. He knew the marriage with Sir Richard loomed on the horizon but in typical optimism believed it to be set for 1573.

One December morning when he was riding in a very leisurely fashion down through the woods at Chelsea, he ran into a gay hunting party of brightly dressed

young men and women. He judged them to be
courtiers; their air of privilege and a degree of hauteur
confirmed that. His eye was caught by one young
woman – brilliant blue eyes, petite features, including a
delightful retroussé nose and bright red lips. She
turned carelessly as he reined his horse in off the track
to let her pass and she looked through him.

The lady was dressed in the height of fashion. She
wore a high gable head-dress of dark crimson with
falling lappets of contrasting pink, finely embroidered.
Her jet black hair was tightly rolled, just revealed above
the high white forehead and delicately winged
eyebrows. Her overgown was also of the finest crimson
velvet, which fell in heavy folds over the white brocaded
dress, heavily embroidered in saffron and pink. The
sleeves were of the new fashion, slashed to reveal the
cream chemise, and were peeping from below the
heavily padded and embroidered velvet wings of the
overgown. She was so slender that the total impression
was one of delicacy, despite the richness of the apparel.
She wore beautiful finely fringed leather gloves and
entrancing decorated shoes. She was just perched on
her tall black mare, but rode with ease and elegance.
Nicholas was overwhelmed. It was a memory that he was
to carry with him for many a day. For Nicholas loved the
mysterious, the unknown, the challenge. It was to make
him a good servant to Walsingham and a restless and
unsatisfactory husband.

Indeed increasing restlessness at hanging around the
shipyards drove Nicholas in late January to consider an
appeal to Walsingham for immediate employment. As
he pondered this on the slow journey back to lodgings
in Cheapside, he realised that a final decision had to be
made about Margaret. He longed for her; the contrast
between the calm exterior and the hidden passion
intrigued him. She loved him, of that he had no doubt,
but he did question whether or not Sir Henry would

permit a match unless he had more evidence of some fortune or hope of it. Depression hung over the winter scene: a swirling ground mist, bare branches dripping icy water in a slow thaw, all served to contribute to Nicholas' own view of his fortunes. It was one of the very few occasions when his natural optimism seemed to have deserted him. He was concerned to arrive back at Cheapside in the pitch dark, as the London streets were notoriously unsafe. Sourly, he thought that the thieves would gain little profit from attacking him! As he led his horse into the stables he was astounded to find Margaret's groom, Will, waiting, and grinning from ear to ear. 'Master, the Mistress Bourne requests you return to High Coombe immediately.'

'I know no Mistress Bourne, Will. Give over, man. You make no sense.'

In his excitement, Will's words came tumbling out. 'Sir Richard married our mistress in December; by New Year's Day he was dead, thrown from his horse. Mistress is distressed and bids you return,' this with a sly look and chuckle.

Nicholas threw his cap over the rafters of the ancient stable and did the high-stepping trip of a fashionable galliard. Margaret was his – and her fortune with her. With this thought, he recalled Sir Richard's wealth and estates at Bourne.

'By God, Will, take a cup of malmsey with me before we return tomorrow.'

'Yes, sir,' said Will, glowing with the thought that the new master was so appreciative. Nicholas was being invited back as the new husband. Will was convinced that this was what his message portended.

Margaret was waiting by the gatehouse as Nicholas and Will rode in three weeks later. She was already visibly with child and came forward carefully over the icy cobbles. She threw herself into his arms as he dismounted. 'Nicholas. Oh, Nicholas. You have come home.'

3   Eden

It had taken Nicholas several days to unravel the full story of the months since he had left. Two things had astounded him. The fact that, unbeknown to everyone except Rachel, the child that Margaret was carrying was his. Nicholas was conceited enough never to doubt this. Curiously though, he did not welcome it. He was always to resent Kit's existence as though Margaret had not married him for himself but to father her child. It was totally illogical since Kit's father, in law, was her first husband Sir Richard Bourne. Secondly, he was surprised that Margaret had been adamant that she would marry Nicholas. No amount of pressure could lessen her resolve. A considerable heiress in her own right, with the Bourne estates and fortune added, (for Richard had died childless, apart from the one in her womb), she could challenge her father's guardianship and appeal to the courts. Sir Henry could not see all that combined land going out of the family, for Sir Richard's lands lay alongside his own. So he gave in to his daughter and allowed her to send for Nicholas.

Sir Henry's hostility to Nicholas melted in the months after the quiet and hasty wedding – a wedding which provoked shocked gossip in the neighbourhood. Margaret, in deference to Richard, wore mourning. It tended to disguise the length of pregnancy anyway. In this way also, she kept away from neighbours and friends. They were all invited to a great celebration for the Bourne heir in July, and such was the power and wealth of the new dynasty that the scandal was put away. No-one in the county wanted to exclude themselves from the patronage and influence of Sir Henry and his new son-in-law.

Sir Henry noticed how quickly Nicholas was accepted. His charm, virility and gregarious nature endeared him to his neighbours, especially to the women. So although Sir Henry had forgiven him, he viewed askance Nicholas' approach to the most attractive members of the opposite sex.

However, Nicholas had waited on Margaret during the later months of pregnancy, paced the Great Chamber in anxiety whilst she was in labour as any good husband would. He had leapt the stairs three at a time, not to clasp his son to his heart, but rather his exhausted and exultant wife.

'Margaret, oh Margaret, you are safe. I kept thinking, what shall I do if she dies?'

His wife looked up at him with adoring eyes. 'Nicholas, do you really love me and need me as much as that?' Then she added, 'This is *your* son. Take him to your heart, for he is your heir.'

Roughly, Nicholas thrust away his wife's hands from the cradle where they rested. He spared the baby no more than a cursory glance, despite the fact that he was stamped with the Carew heritage. In a few days the astounding likeness to Elizabeth Carew Vigus faded. Anyway, Christopher Trenow Bourne was soon banished to a wet nurse and a nursery despite Margaret's pleas.

Only after Nicholas' death did Kit learn that the negligent man who hardly noticed his existence was in fact his natural father. It was a heritage that was to bear bitter fruit.

But, for Margaret, the summer of 1573 was to be the happiest of her life. Nicholas was an attentive and passionate husband. Night after night she responded to his fervent attentions with a loving all her own. His experience, added to her sensuality, gave them hours of pleasure. She never tired of his firm muscled body, nor he of her fine breasts and curvaceous limbs. Her skin was of apricot warmth, the small hands which wandered all over his body were white, soft, warm and infinitely seductive. By the autumn Margaret knew that she was pregnant again; to her great surprise Nicholas seemed overjoyed and set his sights on a daughter.

Nicholas' greatest delight was in the horses. they were fortunate in having an Arab strain and Nicholas' black stallion 'Prince' was a great stud and his foals were to bring more wealth to their ever expanding fortunes. The wine trade was flourishing: Nicholas was taking an interest in shipbuilding. The house at Bourne was let to a newcomer to the county, Robert Fursdon, he whose ships were on the stocks at Topsham. But the bulk of the Bourne land, together with that of the Penhale estate was enclosed and given over to sheep. Margaret continued to superintend the wool business, together with her father. She paid close attention to the shearers, had much of the spinning done locally on the estate. Unexpectedly, Sir Henry's health declined. He seemed able to let go – content that at last the estates could manage without him. His time went to young Kit who grew rapidly into a beautiful toddler with russet hair, whose continuing likeness to Elizabeth Carew Nicholas failed to notice.

For in June 1574 and with great ease, Margaret gave birth to Elizabeth Carew Trenow. From the moment she clasped her father's thumb with a tiny hand, he was lost. He carried the baby from room to room; she was a happy and contented child who never cried but was alert to all around her. At night Kit bellowed, waiting in vain for his mother to soothe his teething pains. But Nicholas was jealous of the attention which Margaret gave to her son. By day she was often to be found in the nursery, singing to him and holding him close when he was fretful. At night she belonged to Nicholas and Nicholas alone. Again and again Nicholas came upon mother and son and, frowning, dragged her forth to ride over the estate, to superintend the births of endless foals or to engage in the chase, one of Nicholas' favourite pastimes. It was a summer of blue skies and bright sunshine. To please Nicholas, there were great parties and feasting – celebrations for Elizabeth's birth and christening. As Autumn approached, great hunts were arranged. New falcons were trained and new huntsmen taken on. Even merchants came from as far afield as Exeter and Plymouth to partake of the abundant hospitality of High Coombe. The courtyards and stables reverberated with the comings and goings of fine visitors. The Great Hall was used every day – the tables piled with beef, pork, venison, pigeons, conies, heronshaw, quails, delicacies of all kinds, including pastries of wild berries, marchpanes and fruit jellies.

Free from pregnancy for a few months, Margaret rode out each day on her high-spirited mare. She really did not care much for dress, but noting Nicholas' interest, she began to have elaborate gowns. A neighbour, the Lady Eleanor Fursdon, newly come from Court, was there to advise her on these gowns, designed in the very latest fashion. Her High Coombe seamstresses learnt how to embroider the rich fabrics which Nicholas imported for their use. He lavished jewels upon her. Some found their way into the elaborate collars and overskirts; others adorned her person. He had a good income from the horse-breeding, which she had made over to him. Extravagant, he spent his own little hoard of gold coins, so that his own person was richly clothed in brocades and silks. The young couple were the envy of the surrounding countryside.

Suddenly, like the great storm which struck at the height of their initial courtship, all lay in ruins. Margaret was busy supervising the two babies and was in the east wing where the nurseries lay. Nicholas had no patience with any disturbance at night, for he had not ceased to make love to Margaret on as many occasions as possible. Much as she adored her children, Nicholas' needs came first, so the children's rooms were at a considerable distance from her bedchamber: After several hours of play with the children, she felt unexpectedly dizzy and faint. With a secret smile to herself, she guessed correctly that she was in for another pregnancy so, without precedent, she withdrew to her bed to recover without fuss or notice. She knew Nicholas disliked illness or indeed anything which interfered with his pleasure, so she was anxious to keep her condition to herself for as long as possible.

Margaret hummed to herself as she walked quickly from room to room, which, at this time of day, tended to be deserted. Many of the servants were busy at work out of doors on this fine May morning in 1575. She thought that she heard laughter and voices, flung open the door of the great bedchamber. Out of the corner of her eye she saw the great tapestries flutter in the draught – Diana the huntress drew back her bow. But her eyes were drawn to the bed where she saw her husband on top of a flurry of petticoats and bare legs. Margaret clutched the bedpost and one of the nursery maids, a pretty little dark creature called Susannah, caught sight of her over Nicholas' shoulder. 'Oh, madam,' she cried, whilst still engaged with her master. With a hearty curse, Nicholas flung himself off the other side of the bed to stand and stare at his wife in horror. The maid ran, head down, from the room.

Without a word Margaret turned and ran after her, not, as the girl believed, to catch her, for she gave no thought to the unfortunate creature, but Margaret's

whole determination was to escape, be away from the
pain, the humiliation. Still very young, barely eighteen,
she had never considered the possibility that Nicholas
did not love her or that he would ever in his life be
unfaithful. The ingenuous young girl, innocent and
inexperienced, received a terrible shock. the romance
and passion that had survived Nicholas' sudden
departure to London, in the belief that chivalry would
not permit the penniless adventurer to ask for her
hand, were despatched in a moment of folly on her
husband's part.

Nicholas had been so careful. He and his neighbour,
young Robert Fursdon, had gone cautiously to Exeter
from time to time, their wives simultaneously in late
pregnancy. A village maid in the remoter portions of
the estate caught his eye from time to time. In this
instance, he had not marked Susannah until a month or
so ago, but her dark prettiness recalled his mystery
maiden of the Chelsea Woods. This was not the first
occasion that he had tumbled her, but normally they
had found a dark corner of a barn or stable. Bitterly, he
recalled another tumble in another barn. God's truth
why had he not been more careful? He knew the
answer, that he was becoming increasingly bored with
life at High Coombe. The restlessness was back, the
need for new pastures. Margaret was too sweet, too
ready for submission, too eager to give him all he
wanted. He was a man who enjoyed the opposition, the
conquest, as he had the initial reluctance of Susannah to
betray the mistress whom she admired.

To Nicholas' chagrin, Margaret was absent for two
days, so that the servants were agog. His amorous
adventures had been noted and accepted. No-one
expected him to be a faithful husband. His recent visit
to Court and his earlier adventures at sea, fighting the
Spaniards, endeared him to his countrymen, most of
whom were imbued with his own fiery patriotism and

love of the Virgin Queen. They recognised an adventurer when they saw one – a careless and generous master, quick to overlook faults and to offer a tankard or two, however inappropriate the occasion. They liked him without respecting him.

The mistress was different. Reared from birth to a gentle courtesy toward her tenants and servants, her warm serene nature made her an admired figure for miles around. They recognised that their prosperity rested in her capable hands, that her strong sense of justice always prevailed. They knew their place and they felt their work appreciated. No-one knew where she had gone on her new chestnut mare, but they feared for her.

Great was the relief when she rode in one morning two days later. The mare appeared rested (Margaret was as careful of her horses as she was her servants). Nicholas and the household were puzzled by Jess' absence, for the little spaniel was her shadow. The dog had fallen foul of a great farm stallion in the unfamiliar surroundings of Bourne. Poor Margaret! The dog's death was symbolic of her love. All waited for an explanation of Margaret's absence and Jess' disappearance. She gave none to her father, who was the most anxious of all and, seated over their late meal, she seemed to address her husband as if nothing had happened.

Nicholas knew differently. Where a girl had fled from him, a woman returned. In her eyes, no longer soft, he read a great anger, the product of a great hurt. In deference to her immense dignity, he waited until they retired to bed.

In his usual optimistic frame of mind, he believed that he was already forgiven. He did not know his wife; in all the years to come he underrated her: her intelligence, strength of character and her popularity with other people. Nicholas could always deceive himself: he believed that the servants sided with him and laughed at their mistress's innocent expectations. He saw himself as irresistible. So he went to sweep Margaret into his arms. 'Sweetheart, it was nothing. She decoyed me, artful minx. I will dismiss her. Oh Margaret, you know that I adore you. You have cast a spell over me, you witch. This stupid servant girl means nothing, an afternoon's sport. I did not think. It shall not happen again. I love only you – your hair, your skin, your beautiful hands, your adorable mouth. Come let me show you how I feel about that mouth.' He leant over to draw her to him.

'Nicholas. I am no silly girl now. I may well have been in the past. I have been ensnared by your fine talk and your wonderful body. But *you* are not wonderful. You are a treacherous deceiver. If she is only a silly servant girl, she is my servant, all the more to be pitied for her stupidity in being decoyed by her master. I, her mistress, shall protect her. She shall stay and you will go.' Then she added with bitterness, 'Get you to the stews in Exeter, where you have defiled our marriage before now.'

Nicholas turned away, puzzled by her words. How had she known of his local exploits? Suddenly he realised that Margaret must have fled to their neighbours, the Fursdons, over in the great house at Bourne. For only a few months before Elizabeth's birth they had leased the enormous mansion to a young man, Robert Fursdon, who had rapidly become an important influence in Nicholas' life and his boon companion.

Robert's origins were in some ways very similar to Nicholas' own, but in other ways they were entirely different, for Robert was the youngest son of loving parents who were devoted to each other and to him, but they were poor Cornish fisherfolk. Robert had gone to sea almost as soon as he could walk, helping his elderly father with the boat, the nets and a variable harvest of

fish. It was a precarious living and the family often
starved. When Robert was only fourteen, his parents
had both been carried off by a low fever. Robert had
vowed then, when he looked for the last time at the
emaciated bodies of his mother and father, that he
would never go hungry again. He had left his village
and his brothers and sisters, all of whom were
considerably older than himself, and at Falmouth he
had been taken on as a sailor on an Indies-bound
privateer. Even at fourteen he was tall for his age,
although thin from near-starvation. Life at sea
hardened his muscles and filled out his large frame and,
by early manhood he stood nearly six foot tall with
massive shoulders and legs like trunks of trees. Friends
likened him to bluff King Hal, although he was swarthy
where the King was fair. A fine dark curly beard and a
shock of black hair masked his rather coarse features,
which were enlivened by sparkling eyes and tanned
skin. Like Nicholas, he returned from the sea in
possession of some fortune, which he promptly invested
in a small ship of his own. He went into partnership with
an old man who had traded for years with The
Netherlands in woollen cloth: it was Robert who
discovered that salt was an excellent return cargo and
who had set up panneries close to his old village,
providing employment for the local population. He was
soon into tin mining as well and so delighted was his
new partner with the young man's energy and drive that
he left him his share of the partnership when he died.
But he had bequeathed him more than that, for Robert
had used the old man to acquire a rudimentary
education in reading and writing, in book-keeping and
in the manners of a gentleman.

So it was that on his very first expedition to London
Robert found himself confident enough to dine at a
great city merchant's, where he met the Lady Eleanor
Bohun. In her veins ran the blood of Plantagenet kings,

a tainted heritage in so far as interbreeding between first cousins made her a delicate woman, given to sickness. Where Robert was vigorous, the Lady Eleanor was languorous. At this city banquet she was immediately attracted to the cheerful and lively giant who sat across the table from her. He was so different from any other man she had met before. He, in his turn, likened her in his mind to those tiny baby birds whom he was wont to pick up from the ground, when they had fallen or wandered from their nests. Her small fair head dropped upon the long neck and fragile bones of shoulder and chest. Her skin was transparent, revealing the blue veins. Her fine hair was like thistledown and her grey eyes bright. Her voice was low and cultured, her manners exquisite and her appetite like a sparrow's. Whereas Robert ate copiously from every dish, she took a morsel here and there. He drained his tankards of beer and wine; she sipped sparingly.

When Robert began to woo her he could not believe that his suit was accepted by her guardian, the same city merchant in whose house he had dined so fortuitously that night. But the merchant was no fool, the lady was eight years older than her suitor, in her late twenties, her only assets a small estate and a rotting castle in Buckinghamshire. For the first time the Lady Eleanor was enthusiastic about a prospective bridegroom. However, her Plantagenet forbears drew Robert; he was very ambitious and foresaw a Fursdon dynasty with both wealth and status.

Robert was always to prove sensitive to others and he wooed the lady with care. He did not hurry her into marriage: consequently, she fell deeply in love with him. He informed her guardian that he would find a suitable house for his bride, if he would consent to the alliance. Bourne was not for sale but Robert met Nicholas and negotiated a lease. He took to Robert immediately and awaited his return from London with great eagerness.

Margaret, in her turn, befriended the Lady Eleanor, introducing her to the locality. She found her new neighbour difficult. At first she put her withdrawn manner down to arrogance. Gradually the Lady Eleanor began to talk and one afternoon, three months after her arrival at Bourne, as they sat in one of the many arbours in the hillside garden at Bourne, she confessed to Margaret that she was pregnant once again, and terrified of it. Margaret had seen the deference with which Robert's high-born wife was treated and she had watched the lady's exquisite manners. She herself had never been further than Exeter and was frightened of being a bumpkin in Eleanor's eyes. But she now saw beneath the fine gowns and jewels, with which Robert proudly bedecked his wife, a frightened woman, hopelessly in love with her husband. Margaret's kindess and protective manner drew Eleanor to her and they became close friends. So it was she who advised Margaret on dress and fashion and Nicholas assumed that Eleanor had told Margaret of the visits which Robert and he paid to whores in Exeter. Indeed, Robert's wife had befriended Margaret during the two days in which she absented herself from Nicholas and High Coombe.

Eleanor was no innocent, a worldly woman reared in the shadow of Court and a dangerous Plantagenet heritage, aware that Robert Fursdon had married her for his own advancement. She adored her husband but recognised his many faults. She tried to get Margaret to recognise that Nicholas was human and no worse for that. Eleanor had hoped that Margaret's anger would evaporate, given time.

But it had not, and Nicholas was also proud. Stung with the words, 'She is *my* servant,' conscious always of his position as consort, he met anger with anger.

'Madam, I have long neglected my duties at Court, to the Queen, still in danger from her Catholic foes. I shall leave at first light.'

Margaret was aware of the interview with Walsingham and Nicholas' hopes. She had assumed that, with all that she could offer Nicholas, they would be forgotten. She had paid little attention to Nicholas' proud assertion of the Queen's need of him.

Worn out by the strain of keeping up appearances, by the fierce anger that consumed her, and by the vagaries of early pregnancy, she had left the bedchamber and gone back to the children's room; unable to bear even the thought of the violence of Nicholas' demeanour and his harsh words, she fell into an uneasy sleep. Her last thought was: I can cope better in the morning. But in the morning he had gone.

4 New Friends

Margaret's pregnancies had been easy; twinges of early morning nausea in the early months had been followed by a general sense of well-being. But this pregnancy, especially after Nicholas' departure, was different. Margaret found it very hard to eat, to walk and to sleep. She was perpetually sick and had violent headaches. She wondered whether the general malaise was due to her condition or to the sense of anger, loss and indeed guilt in the months following the rejection of her husband.

At one time, Margaret might well have mounted her horse and pursued him, as she knew the route he would surely take to London. She knew his lodgings, discovered by Will early in 1573. She did nothing. She wondered at her own reactions. Did she no longer love him? Was love so easily banished? Susannah's obvious pregnancy was a constant reminder of the cause. Yet early training and concern for her servants, together with pride, forbade her to send the girl away. She knew Susannah's family would not accept her. Sometimes, pride that the 'droit de seigneur' had been exercised prompted estate or village families to display their bastards openly. But, in Susannah's case, the family were strict Puritans.

Susannah's natural gaiety was now suppressed, possibly for ever. She crept around the house, refusing absolutely to discuss the affair with any of her fellows. Her only solace was in the two children, Kit and

Elizabeth. She spurned the attentions of Will, who had always been attracted to the sweet little creature since her arrival at High Coombe. After Alice's birth in November, however, Susannah reverted to her normal somewhat irresponsible self and, in December, she gladly consented to marry Will. He had negotiated a new position at Bourne, with Margaret's ready consent, but on one condition. For Susannah's mistress insisted that Nicholas' daughter must be reared alongside his other children, receiving the same education and privileges. It was typical of Margaret that it never crossed her mind to question Alice's parentage then or at any time in the future, although, in fact, the tiny blonde fairylike creature she grew into bore no resemblance to any of Nicholas' family or to Nicholas himself.

During these months preceding Alice's birth, Margaret's depression deepened. She vomited every morning and often during the day. She was thin and pale, the pregnancy scarcely visible. She was given to fits of dizziness and severe headaches. Lady Eleanor Fursdon was in little better condition herself, but she and Margaret visited each other at frequent intervals. Concern for her friend prompted Eleanor to send for Nicholas. The messenger arrived at Cheapside to find Nicholas had unexpectedly departed for Kenilworth. It was a stupendous stroke of luck for him that he had run into his old patron, Sir John Gauldnay. He was an easy-going old man and much taken with Nicholas' charm so that he invited him to join his train, which was following the Queen's visit to her favourite, the Earl of Leicester. Sir John noted Nicholas' rich apparel in the latest fashion, the heavily slashed doublet and hose in rich gold and russet, the short collarless Spanish cloak, richly embroidered in dark green, the bonnet adorned with ostrich and osprey feathers, the cross gartering and embroidered shoes. Indeed Nicholas was now completely at home in the brilliant Court assemblage, reinforced with his wife's fortunes, which he could draw on in London. He rode one of the finest mares which High Coombe had produced, a fine large chestnut creature with a cream mane and a fine Arab head. It was this animal which first drew the attenion of the Lady Letitia Tilney, whose entourage had met up with Sir John's near Leicester.

So it was that Nicholas found himself riding into Kenilworth alongside the lady of his dreams, whom he had seen in the Chelsea Woods. Her spouse was an influential courtier and an easy-going husband.

The days of Kenilworth flew by in heat and sunshine. He lingered by her side, content to fetch and carry, escorting her to the play given by the men of Coventry, since her husband was afflicted with sunstroke.

They laughed together at the antics of the Warwickshire yokels, whose broad vowels they could scarcely understand. When Adam and Eve were in Eden, Adam kept turning to the back of the platform to say out loud, 'Is the Devil ready? Has he his serpent's clothes?'

Letitia's high-pitched tones began to annoy those around them, so, bored with the familiarity of the New Testament scenes, they made their way down to the river and to Nicholas' delight he and Letitia were alone at last. He was allowed to caress her white neck and bosom, to cover her with kisses. When he would go further, she said petulantly, 'La, Nicholas, I have to return to Court and cannot appear with creased clothes and loose curls like some Warwickshire dairymaid.' Indeed Nicholas was in his element, for thanks to Letitia's position they attended the Queen's picnic in the woods, where the Queen herself was languid in love for the handsome Robert Dudley, exquisitely clothed in the most elaborate of doublets, his fine silk hose displaying his handsome legs to perfection. All the ladies loved him; Lady Letitia's dark lashes fell flirtatiously over the great blue eyes. Her elaborately embroidered silver

French farthingale made her waist look even smaller. The colour set off the pink and white complexion. The slender neck and shoulders were enhanced by an enormous ruff beneath which a daring décolletage revealed a snowy bosom. Her fingers were adorned with a multitude of rings, and rivalled the Queen's own renowned hands in their alabaster whiteness. Nicholas' mood was one of ecstasy, despite the fact that his only reward for his constant attention was one virginal kiss. When the Lady Eleanor's messenger arrived, Nicholas was dismayed. He could not withdraw his courtship at such a favourable stage. Apart from anything else, the Tilneys were long-standing courtiers of repute with useful connections who could forward his career. Then Nicholas had an inspiration. He despatched one of his most faithful henchmen, an ugly grizzled seaman called Luke

In fairness, his anger with Margaret had long since evaporated. He was amused by her naiveté and now put her distress down to the vagaries of a pregnant woman. But he was concerned for her well-being and hit upon the idea of sending his favourite sister, Felicity, to put things to rights. Felicity could assure Margaret of Nicholas' devotion to his wife and family, and of the upward turn in his fortune. He was not remiss at showing his success by despatching a generous gift of gold to his sister in the hands of this messenger, who was commissioned to escort Felicity to High Coombe and there to take up residence till his master's return.

Luke had lost an arm in Drake's 1572 expedition to the Indies: he had some money in his own right, but was seeking a comfortable and secure billet, where he could live out the rest of his life. He admired Nicholas for his swaggering vigour and relied upon his open-handedness in the future. Luke reasoned that a man serving Walsingham and linked to Drake and Hawkins, married to a wealthy West Country heiress, could only be in the ascendant. So Luke carried the message and the money, arriving at Felicity's farm in September.

Felicity was both flattered and alarmed. She had never met her brother's wife, but had come by news of Nicholas via neighbours and servants of the local gentry. Felicity had not received Nicholas' education, her mother Elizabeth Carew Vigus was a lady born and had taught her only daughter manners and customs of that class. So Felicity was an odd mixture and had always found a conflict in the demands, attitude and lifestyles of her yeoman husband Tom Gray and her own secret social aspirations.

Nicholas' gold was a godsend and, at the same time, offered a channel for those very aspirations. Difficult as it was to leave, she being a working farmer's wife, Felicity persuaded a cousin, on substantial payment, to stand in for her. All the way across from Dartmoor she rehearsed what she might say. She might have allayed her fears had she known the circumstances of her arrival, since Margaret was ripe for a new friendship and for support. Felicity's humble beginnings and appearance would be ignored.

Lady Eleanor had sustained Margaret in the early months of pregnancy but Lady Eleanor was now too ill herself with a fifth pregnancy in five years, and she was in her late thirties.

Sir Henry's hostility to his son-in-law had returned on Nicholas' hasty departure in 1575. Sir Henry's servants were loyal to him and he knew about his son-in-law's activities. He resented it on his daughter's behalf, but, more importantly, saw himself duped by a penniless rogue. The old man had a seizure in May, soon after Nicholas left for London. There is no doubt that his poor health had helped to deter Margaret from leaving her babies and the estate to pursue her husband to London.

So when Felicity arrived in October, she found all in

confusion. Winter preparations were being made, but servants and tenants alike lacked firm guidance. Margaret had taken to her bed a month gone and refused to see anyone but her old friend and servant Rachel.

Felicity's early training stood her in good stead. Small in stature, plump with frequent childbearing, clad in homely fustian and astride a nag which had seen better days, escorted by a ruffianly one-armed sailor – the servants eyed her askance and barred her entry. Dismounting and pulling herself up to her full five foot two inches of height, she demanded in a low cultured voice to see her sister-in-law Margaret Trenow. She stood her ground and was reluctantly admitted to the great bedchamber and found Margaret shut in the dark.

Felicity was appalled to see a small, grossly swollen woman apparently in her late thirties. Not only was her body swollen, but her face. Her fine curly chestnut hair was lank and uncombed. Felicity's first thought was, 'No wonder Nicholas had fled to London'. But thoughts of Nicholas brought her to her senses. She curtseyed to Margaret, addressing her as 'Madam' and, spreading her thick skirt, sat down firmly on a nearby chest.

Within days she had Margaret eating and taking exercise. Felicity was experienced, not only in her own pregnancies, but in nursing her mother through eight. She encouraged Margaret to play with her children; she brought her to a returning interest in her estate. Gradually she began to talk to her about Nicholas' childhood. It came to a head one dark evening in early October when all the servants had retired. Outside a wild cold wind and heavy rain buffeted the windows and sent the branches of giant elms crashing to the ground. Inside, a great log fire flamed and crackled, sending strange shadows over the wainscoting in the light of a few flickering candles, which spluttered in their turn, adding to the ominous sounds without and within. The two women sat side by side on the oak settle, feet wriggling in front of the fire to secure maximum warmth.

Felicity said, 'Kit bears a remarkable resemblance to my mother. Perhaps that is why Nicholas seems to dislike him.'

'Why? Did Nicholas dislike his own mother?' said Margaret, in awed tones.

'Oh no. He adored her. Unlike my brothers, he would do anything for her. Scour floors, chop wood, carry water. He liked to brush her hair of an evening.'

'How curious then that he has never remarked upon Kit's features.'

'Yes but you must remember that my mother ignored Nicholas, even when he was brushing her hair and he hung upon her every word.'

Margaret's eyes grew round with pity. 'Why, I believed that he and his mother were so close, drawn together by the terrible circumstances of his birth. How did this fine lady manage after Adam Trenow died so tragically?'

'She didn't,' replied Felicity. 'She hated him for it and she hated Nicholas because he had brought her so low. My father took her in and treated her well. She had to work hard around the farm but my father was always kind. I wonder at his patience when they were both so contemptuous of him. Yet curiously it was Elizabeth who beat Nicholas unmercifully, never John Vigus. My mother insisted that Nicholas was tutored, whilst the rest of us never had a chance.' Here a note of bitterness crept in.

Margaret, ever practical, commented, 'But where did the money come from?'

'I think the priest enjoyed teaching such a bright lad and was largely paid in kind. Half these poor clergy starve on the few tithes they get anyway. This cleric was also very musical and Nicholas has great talent there. But oh how the village boys teased Nicholas for it! They chased him and bullied him until he grew big enough to beat them all in turn and became the leader. He was the best swimmer, the best wrestler and finally he could out-drink and out-whore any of them.' She stopped. 'I am sorry, Margaret. I intended no disrespect.'

Margaret had grown fond of Felicity, grateful for her care, support and interest, so she forgave her for those idle words. However, they were perhaps not so idle after all, for in Felicity lay the seeds of a canker which would not only corrupt Felicity but a whole family.

For Felicity was herself beautiful, much more beautiful than Margaret. She had fine features, rich colouring of russet and apricot, with deep green eyes. Pare away the flesh engendered by a series of rapid pregnancies and beneath lay the fine slender bones of her birth, bred as she was out of Elizabeth Carew and generations of aristocrats. In addition she had a delicious voice and her low cultured tones were the produce of her mother's careful schooling.

Felicity saw the coarser Margaret, handsome yet without real beauty, able to make the most of herself because of a great fortune. She went clad in velvet and silk, of rare rich colours, whilst Felicity wore dull fustian. Felicity saw Margaret in command of great estates and a fine house. How her companion envied her that lovely fortress dominating the valley of the Lyn; it was a background for a woman respected by neighbours and tenants. Yet Felicity knew herself to be just as able to command, just as competent and above all far more attractive to men, given the right setting and the rich apparel. Jealousy gnawed at her like some evil growth. As yet, she was hardly aware of it. She sought to stifle the envious twinges and to be a companion and a support to Nicholas' wife.

Margaret had already faced the truth that her

husband was lecherous and unfaithful. Now, in further talks with her sister-in-law, she explored the bitterness of his childhood. the insults, the taunts and finally the perpetual lack of affection on his mother's part. She saw the pride and selfishness in Elizabeth Vigus and she was to recognise it later in her own daughter.

Meanwhile, Margaret learnt how this strong youth, renowned for his physical prowess, joined the village lads not only in wild poaching adventures and also down to the coast aboard the fishing vessels. For Nicholas loved the sea and, aged fourteen, had run off to seek his fortune to bring it back for his mother, to enable her once again to live the life of a lady, to wear fine clothes, ride well-bred horses, hunt and entertain.

Felicity was sad as she recited Nicholas' confidences, for Felicity was his only friend in the family. He scorned John Vigus, as Elizabeth scorned him. 'Nicholas has to prove himself to himself,' Felicity said slowly, 'as well as to others. He has stood alone all his life. I believe that he loves me; I know that he loves you, but always he needs other women. They make him feel important; they cosset him and flatter him.' Margaret began to admit to herself, although not to Felicity, that she had never understood her husband. He had met her requirements – his virility first and foremost. Then he had been the handsome and charming helpmeet, who was the lover and husband of her dreams. She had seen his needs only in terms of status and fortune; she had been proud that she and she only could satisfy them. Then she began to understand why he was desperate to succeed at Court, to win a fortune possibly in adventuring at sea. He must prove himself a man. But Margaret failed to understand that Elizabeth Carew's death, far from solving a problem had exacerbated it, for Nicholas sought to win his mother's approbation, in death as in life. It was an impossible dream.

Felicity left, satisfied that she had carried out

Nicholas' orders. In late November, after a difficult and dangerous confinement, Margaret gave birth to twin boys, one of whom, Thomas, died a week later. Nobody, except Rachel, who nursed him continuously and devotedly, gave Timothy, the other child, much prospect of life.

Margaret's hopes now lay with her husband. She loved the new frail baby but she was returning to life and she refused to mourn her son. She recovered very quickly; her physical stamina was great and now, thanks to Felicity, her courage and faith were returning also. It was just as well, for in December her father died and the West Country faced its worst winter for twenty years.

Whilst in Devon the snow fell heavily and without cease for two weeks in late December, Nicholas was enjoying the French Court.

After his idyllic weeks in Kenilworth, Nicholas had been invited to the Tilneys' fine house in Nottinghamshire. But his suit got no further than a kiss or two and he grew impatient to return to Court. The decision was finally made when he received an invitation to make a call on Walsingham. He realised his luck when Walsingham invited him to find out the true state of affairs at the French Court. For the Queen's erstwhile suitor, the Duc d'Anjou, was now King Henry III.

It was a complicated political situation where the King's heir, Henry of Anjou, was already linked to the Huguenots and possibly the Duke of Orange. The last outcome desired by the Queen was an alliance of Catholic France with the Protestants. The English Queen knew that she stood alone, her title challenged by the Roman Catholics who refused to recognise the marriage of her parents. Should the Protestants in Europe join her Catholic enemies, she was lost. The danger to the Queen from an assassin's dagger was constantly present. Nicholas saw his ambition and his patriotism come together in this new project. When he arrived in France, the corruption and scheming, the deceit, worried him not at all. Elizabeth Carew might have taught him manners but her bitterness about the course which her own life had taken had bred in him a lack of respect for human beings, a total lack of trust and faith in anything other than original sin. A curious mixture of self-confidence and a deep sense of inferiority made Nicholas a difficult man to understand. French men acknowledged his charm and courtesy, women his chivalry and sexual prowess. It was a combination that went down well in Court circles. As a result, he managed to pick up a great deal of information about the secret intentions of the King and his advisors. He learnt about the religious struggle, about the superficiality of reconciliations between Huguenot and Catholic. He was to tell Walsingham that the repercussions of the massacre of St. Bartholomew of 1572 would last a century or more. Men and women were indiscreet in his presence, as he was judged to be a likeable and harmless courtier, greedy for advancement and gold, but lacking both intelligence and principle. No hint of his patriotism was to emerge and, anyway, Frenchmen did not understand the English courtiers' devotion to their Queen. He returned to London in the spring of 1576; Walsingham was always reserved and the lack of monetary reward in the Queen's service was notorious. But Nicholas was amply compensated by a further introduction to the Queen herself. He lingered at Court, seeking, in vain, Lady Letitia's pretty face and figure.

5 The Long Winter

On her way to full recovery, Margaret was only too well aware of the neglect of house and estate. the servants were well-meaning: the steward, major-domo and bailiff had done their best but a strong hand, with a knowledge of over-all policy and objectives, was always needed. In fact, Margaret realised that although her father had trained his daughter, preparation for responsibility in others was lacking. Sir Henry's ways had not kept pace with the enormous expansion of his possessions during his lifetime.

The priority was not within the house, nor even the kitchen, great as was Margaret's desire to set all to rights immediately. She turned her attention to the home farm: the slaughtering policy in terms of numbers had been faithfully pursued, but insufficient notice had been taken of a poor summer and a consequently poor yield of winter fodder. Reluctantly the new mistress ordered further slaughter and sent off down the coast for more salt. She sent the bailiff on to supervision of this major task, in the windy wet weather of mid-December 1575.

It was fortunate that in the wake of Sir Henry's death, no-one in the neighbourhood expected more from the great house than a desultory recognition of Christmas and New Year festivities. Still only eighteen years of age, the full responsibility of the estate and the family fell upon Margaret, who rode out to the borders of the estates to speak to all her shepherds about the necessity for checking all the flocks. They were always folded as late as possible but the many small valleys and rolling hills of Bourne and High Coombe hid small pockets of valuable sheep. There were many good shepherds, but a few sheep always managed to wander off. Naturally Margaret did no more than indicate likely areas of omission: she could ride her lands blindfold, even the newly acquired Bourne territories, for with Sir Richard's indulgence she had ridden and hunted over them since early childhood.

So it was that, in the second week of January, Margaret decided to check on the activities of some elderly tenants in the valley of the river Yeld. The old couple had lost most of their offspring in early childhood and their two remaining sons had turned wild and gone off to sea. Old Jacob did his best, together with one good shepherd, but Margaret was determined to see for herself the condition of the land and sheep. Her escort of many years, Will, had departed, with his wife Susannah, in early December. The other men were needed in the new urgent activities initiated by Margaret. At first it was her intention to ride alone, but aware that she was only recently risen from child-bed, she decided to call out Nicholas' man, Luke. He played no part in agricultural activities, nor had he shown himself about the house. Margaret was undecided about him: she found his coarse features disturbing and his manner bordering upon the insolent. On this occasion he showed apathy regarding her order to ride out.

To her surprise, a companionable conversation developed and she gained a new insight into many of Nicholas' activities. In no way did Luke betray any confidences, but his accounts of life at sea and of Court life and intrigues were racy and amusing. So absorbed was she that Margaret failed to notice the lowering clouds and hill mist which were descending. Her companion drew her attention to this as they rode into the deserted farmyard of Franscombe. Margaret was impressed with the way Luke managed his horse with one arm and with the speed with which he dismounted to help her down.

Old Mrs Jacob Trelawney came forward, curtseying and inviting them into the warmth of the kitchen. 'My husband is way up the valley bringing down our second flock, as Matthew the shepherd is laid low with the flux.'

Tempting as was the warm kitchen and its great glowing hearth, Margaret and Luke stopped only to snatch a tankard of warm ale, ready mulled for old Jacob's return. They rode into the wind, up the valley, as the first snowflakes descended slowly. They rode fast but steadily. Fortunately, on the lower water meadows the ground was still relatively soft and the air clearer than on the darkening hills. At Luke's suggestion, Mrs Jacob had released one of her dogs. Margaret was given some directions but thought that once they reached the head of the valley 'Tod' might lead them to his master with greater accuracy than they could achieve on their own.

Margaret was always to remember Luke's continuing good humour in these hours when, as an old sailor, he was already sensing the hazards of the weather. He had indicated them to her and left it at that. In her turn, she told him of Jacob's increasing infirmities and her interest in Jacob's fine flocks, as this valley was excellent sheep country. They did not discover the old man until late afternoon and the weather was truly formidable by that time. The wind howled in from the north, the snow falling intermittently, but heavier by the hour. With luck, Jacob had got the sheep on to a lower track, sheltered by oak woodlands. It had always been Sir Henry's policy to save his oaks. He knew their value but regarded them as insurance for any sudden drop in wool prices.

Jacob was by now so exhausted that Margaret was about to give him her mare. Luke insisted on dismounting, pointing out that he could the more easily walk, as he was not impeded by heavy petticoats. Even here, their sense of humour exerted itself and Margaret and Luke exchanged amused glances. But both horses were exhausted by the long ride and made restive by the creaking and cracking of the boughs, so Jacob was hoisted, sack-like, on to the saddle of Luke's sturdy mount, whilst Margaret led both horses. The dogs were steady with a flock that ran, distressed, down towards Franscombe. When they emerged from the wood, they were met with blinding snow and the inability to see an inch or so before their noses.

They paused, holding the sheep in. There were two alternatives. To keep themselves and the sheep safely for the night in the shelter of the trees. It would be cold but all could huddle together for warmth. If they did this, they risked being marooned in the midst of snowdrifts next morning. The temperature was still falling. They could try going on, chancing the senses of the animals, as well as Margaret's knowledge of the land, to guide them blindfold over the next mile or so. Luke was for staying but Margaret's memories of these hills in heavy snow drove her on. At least she had the river and its subsidiary as some kind of marker.

In the early hours of the morning they reached the farm, certain that some beasts had been lost by the wayside. The dogs had been reluctant to press on and leave the strays in the flock, but Jacob was not so far gone that from horseback he could not still command the sheepdogs. Even at Franscombe they could not just drop into the kitchen settles and sleep. Luke and Margaret, with Mrs Jacob's help, found hurdles to fold in the dizzy sheep, who were so bewildered that they might yet have wandered. Those they had saved must be preserved. Then their exhausted mounts were to be rubbed down and securely stabled.

Margaret stumbled into the house and relieved herself of the damp skirts. Modesty was gone, as was the etiquette between mistress and servants. Wrapped in sheepskins, she slept and woke in early daylight to find the snow up the panes of the small farmhouse windows. Luke grinned at her from the other side of the hearth. 'A wise decision, my lady. If we were in those woods now we would be truly sunk.' She noted the maritime phrase and thought that, for a land-lubber, Luke had done well yesterday!

The farmhouse, like most in this part of the country, lay sheltered in the fold of a great hill. When Margaret ventured beyond the farmyard, she found a dazzling but forbidding scene. The surrounding countryside was a blinding white. All the hedges and trees were masked like great ghosts with enormous white fingers and massive stumpy white figures. The tracks were truly covered and although the temperature was low enough for the snow to be crisp, the skies still seemed heavy with a forbidding and lowering grey tone.

This time Luke's advice held sway. 'Although the wind has dropped, my lady, there's more snow to come. If you venture in this, you'll be caught again, but this time there's already a foot of snow at least before the next lot. Anyway, rest ourselves and the horses today. No doubt they will be alarmed at High Coombe but they will hope that you have taken shelter.'

There was indeed little rest, as old Jacob developed a fever and Mrs Jacob was taken up with nursing him. Luke and Margaret worked side by side to feed all the animals before the next fall.

Jacob was old but an experienced farmer, so fodder was found in well-stocked barns. When indeed, by three in the afternoon, the wind was up again and the snow fell as thickly as before, Margaret and Luke retired to the kitchen to find a great platter of bacon and new-made bread spread before them, followed by ewes' cheese. Old-fashioned, home-made cider warmed them in body and spirit. The feeling of vigour and optimism deserted her and Margaret fell into a feverish sleep. For two days old Mrs Jacob nursed her. The valiant Luke was joined by the old shepherd who had been marooned for two days by snow and by the flux.

The days passed slowly, with little abatement in the weather. Luke sought to cheer his mistress with tales of the sea and pirateering. It was all too violent and bloodthirsty for her tastes but it distracted her from the worry about High Coombe and the children. The real danger was that the weather had set in for winter.

At the end of five days, Luke forecast a break. There was no thaw but the sun shone and the overnight frost kept the surface hard and even. Should they risk the horses? It would give them speed but was it practical? A trial run on the Friday proved disastrous. The only hope they had was to negotiate the drifts on foot and to make their way through the valleys, keeping as far as possible close to the water, both as markers and also, where possible, to risk the ice, as preferable to the heavy drifts. Margaret knew of stop-overs and laid careful plans. She had spent the time shut in the farmhouse sewing together some breeches of a sort and she had arrived clad in sturdy leather boots. A great woollen cloak, donated in gratitude by the Trelawny couple, completed her outfit. They carried as much food as they could muster.

Half a mile at a time they negotiated their way, stopping overnight in shepherds' huts and local farmhouses, where they were warmly welcomed and cosseted. In the uninhabited huts, Luke produced a fire with a tinder box brought from Franscombe and, unashamedly, they huddled together for warmth. Margaret's eyes were closed before supper was over and, when she woke, the fire was already going and the snow melted for a hot drink.

The last mile was horrendous; the weather had steadily

worsened in the last two days. the winds roared and the snow scudded across the barely visible track. Only in the woods was it possible to make any time at all. Both knew that this mile had to be done and that more snow was on the way. Finally Luke turned and said, 'My lady, I will go on and bring back help. At this pace, we will not make it before dark.'

'Do you know the way?'

'Yes, I think so. I came down here when I journeyed from London. I have a sailor's instinct. But you must keep walking.' Here Luke's shrewd assessment of his mistress stood him in good stead. 'Remember your children. They need you. Keep going.'

With an amazing burst of energy he was away. With a laugh, at the bend of the hill he blew her a kiss. Hours later, Margaret's men found her huddled under a hedge, protected by one of the great boulders that littered this part of the countryside. She was just breathing.

Old Rachel had her brought in by the fire in the great bedchamber. She lay on heavy rugs before the fire and was cosseted with soup and a posset of herbs. Twenty-four hours later, when she opened her eyes, it was to see the baby Timothy gurgling away next to her. Too tired to speak she smiled weakly at Rachel, nodding her thanks, and fell once again into a deep sleep.

Margaret's recovery was slow but steady. Orders were given from her bed. Fodder was short, fresh meat at a premium. A number of beggars and even local farmers presented themselves at the gates and were assisted. High Coombe survived. Timothy flourished. Luke kept his counsel in a warm corner in the great kitchen. In the first week in March the thaw set in.

PART TWO 1577–1582
Felicity

6   Reconciliation

Robert Fursdon stood in front of the great chimney-piece at High Coombe, drying off his extremely damp clothes. Steam rose from him, giving him a look of unreality, as if at any moment he might disappear in a puff of smoke up the chimney. Margaret smiled to herself at her own conceit. Anything less like a wraith than the burly giant from Bourne would be hard to imagine.

Robert's dark eyes shone from under his heavy brows, black hair curled tightly to a well-shaped head, a wide generous mouth half-hidden by a trim beard complemented a handsome appearance of which the owner was well aware. He was laughing, as he so often did. 'Eleanor was in a rare panic, as though you were not the very last person to succumb to this vile Devon winter. You are the native westerner and must have seen it all before.'

'Not like this,' Margaret replied, yet minimising her adventures of the past months. A more observant man than Robert would have marked Margaret's pallor and loss of weight. Robert merely thought to himself that he had never before noted the attractions of his neighbour's person. She had indeed, for once, heightened her appearance by wearing an orange gown with a fine new russet farthingale in the latest form, foreseeing a stream of visitors now that the weather had relented. Had Nicholas been there and he was not, he

would have appreciated the new maturity in Margaret's
thinner face – more reserve certainly, less joy but a
steadiness of gaze. She was enjoying Robert's humour.
Was it possible that Luke's company was developing this
appreciation? The faithful Luke had become a wag, in
constant attention upon his mistress, and always ready
with a quip to counteract the new reserve. Robert knew
nothing of this but was anxious to impress his wealthy
landlord, who refused utterly to sell him the house at
Bourne.

'It is Kit's heritage,' she said, with a momentary
twinge of conscience, recalling Sir Richard's trust in her.

'It is just,' replied Robert, 'that I cannot abide
Eleanor's great house in Buckinghamshire. Nearer to
London it may be, but a dark, dismal, old-fashioned,
crenellated monstrosity.'

Tactfully but formally, Margaret responded, 'We are
so pleased to have you and Lady Eleanor as our
neighbours and you may have the tenancy for life, but
sell I will not.'

Robert admired decisiveness in a woman and was now
finding the Lady Eleanor sadly lacking – a supine
creature, over-bred and far too submissive for his tastes,
she was yet subjected to his continuing physical
attentions, despite a series of difficult confinements and
resultant sickly offspring. So he turned to Margaret and
invited her to hunt with him next week. 'My birds are
savage, too long confined and needing plenty of
exercise.'

Margaret was young and feeling like her own falcons,
eager for the open air and freedom, so she accepted
with great enthusiasm, sending warm messages to Lady
Eleanor and a promise to ride over soon. When Robert
stayed, bent over her hand, just a fraction longer than
he should, the new Margaret shrugged it off, a little
gratified to find that Robert liked her as a woman, but
she saw no disloyalty to her friend. All men were the

same and to be tolerated in their silly quirks. She had no doubt that her enthusiastic reception of his invitation to the chase had touched Robert's vanity. She liked his openness and his love and knowledge of horses. Although she refused to recognise it, she was lonely.

In the months to come, Margaret drew Robert out on his political life – interested in his activities as a member of Parliament, shocked and yet amused at his stories of members' unruliness in the chamber. Margaret had never discussed politics with Nicholas. He had told her of fashions at Court, of what Walsingham wore rather than what he did. It was flattering that Robert treated her as an equal and that he assumed an understanding of the strong anti-Catholic stance of members of Parliament like himself. As fellow-members visited Bourne and the sickly Lady Eleanor kept more and more to her own rooms, Margaret found herself dining at Bourne, sitting at Robert's right hand. With insight and animation, she discussed the situation in The Netherlands. (Were not her wool interests tied up there?) She revealed a knowledge of French affairs, culled from Luke's accounts. Robert's friends rode away in admiration that he was so well connected with such an attractive and influential lady. This was said with a nudge and a wink and a comment upon Lady Eleanor's protracted absences.

Yet when Nicholas returned one spring morning, his first impression of Margaret was a wholly domestic one, for she was supervising a thorough cleaning of the entire house. The enormous tapestries were hung out. Laundry was festooned in a myriad of heaps beyond the kitchen garden. Chimneys were raked. In the midst, Margaret in a dark fustian gown, chestnut hair well-hidden under a dusty cap. 'Good God,' thought Nicholas, his mind on Lady Letitia. 'Why have I bothered to come?' But he kissed his wife hard upon the mouth and gathered her into his arms. He was not to know the new status of his old servant, Luke, or to realise that Luke had noted the fleeting look of distaste on his master's face when he crossed the threshold of the Great Hall to find Margaret in the midst of her servants.

Luke's admiration for his mistress' conduct in the great storm was to survive the years – a loyalty and a respect so strong that it made Luke totally forego any interests of his own. Luke had been orphaned early and sent into the world to fend for himself. The cruel life at sea had made him independent and tough; only in Margaret's company had he recognised his need for comfort, warmth and security. He thought that nothing could ever again persuade him away from High Coombe. Meanwhile, he bustled around, attending to Nicholas' needs for food and hot water.

It was typical of Nicholas that he should ride over to Bourne that very evening. There was still too much hustle and bustle at home for his comfort. A perfunctory visit to the nursery and a game with the very young Elizabeth soon drove him in boredom to the side of his friend Robert. Unfortunately, Robert was away on business in London and Eleanor so late in pregnancy that she declined to see him. Nicholas was thus in a dark mood when he returned to High Coombe.

Margaret had prepared for Nicholas' return. She had sent for pattern books and the finest materials. She now sought to discipline her unruly hair in padded rolls over her temples. She wore a caul of silver mesh to hold in the heavy chestnut coil at the back of her head. Over this she wore a taffeta pipkin with a feather. She had a gown of dark green, a farthingale in the Spanish style. The bodice was stiff with whalebone and came to a fashionable point over the kirtle; both were of apricot silk heavily embroidered in saffron and dark green. The sleeves were tight at the wrist with a lawn ruff but of a contrasting colour. A high Medici collar gave Margaret great presence but the total effect was of dignity and authority rather than of soft-yielding femnity, which Margaret sought to achieve, in deference to Nicholas' preferred tastes.

Margaret sent the servants away and waited upon him personally. 'I long to hear more of your adventures. Robert tells me that you attended the Queen to Kenilworth.'

Turning sharply, Nicholas said, 'What more has old Robert told you?'

Desperately anxious to placate him at all costs in her newfound sympathy for him, Margaret said, 'Very little. But he does tell Eleanor and I about the Court and the Queen's elaborate dresses and jewels.'

Mollified, now Nicholas responded. 'The progress was unbelievable. People lined the route and cheered themselves hoarse. The Queen looked brilliant, sparkling with jewels, mounted on a great white stallion. Kenilworth was a dream. My Lord of Leicester spent a fortune on the entertainment. There were hunts and picnics every day.' He paused warily, for picnics were a dangerous subject since he might in his enthusiasm refer to a certain beauty, whose company he kept.

But Margaret saved the day, for she was anxious to hear about the politics. 'Did you see Walsingham himself?'

'Indeed, and I was able to render him service when I visited France. Oh, Margaret, you should see the luxury of the French Court, the ambition and wealth of the great nobles, the women in their paint and naked bosoms.'

Wryly, Margaret interrupted, 'You enjoyed that.'

But Nicholas ignored the jibe and went on, 'They are so corrupt, so unpatriotic. Anyone can be bribed. Information was easy to come by.'

'Will the Queen marry a Frenchman?'

'Never,' was Nicholas' emphatic response. 'If she does not marry Leicester, she will marry no-one.'

'Robert says that she dare not marry Leicester since Amy Robsart's death.'

'So old Robert does keep you well-informed. Still he has given you a hand here so I cannot grumble.'

Margaret noted the confidence in her husband's tone. He would never be jealous. He was too certain of his own charm and his prowess in bed. Imperceptibly, she sighed.

But that night when Nicholas took her gently in his arms, roused by the curvaceous body, the perfumed flesh and her quick responses, she forgot her resentment and gave herself over to his passion. For the first time in their married life he took her slowly, stroking every part of her body, sampling her hardening nipples, running his hands over the inside of her thighs, nibbling her cheeks and neck till she cried out, 'Now Nicholas, now!' And he took her again and again that night till she rose in the morning to her household duties dark-eyed and bruised, bone-weary yet ecstatic.

Rachel met her mistress late the next morning with a knowing look and Margaret's open glowing face told her all she needed to know. It lasted no more than three days; at the end of that time, Robert returned to Bourne and the two men rode off to Exeter. This time Margaret had no illusions, but she remembered Felicity's account and steadied her angry response, so that by the time Nicholas returned, she said nothing. More than that, she organised hunting parties, feasts and visits from new neighbours to welcome him back and keep boredom at bay.

It was weeks before he commented upon Alice's presence in the nursery and even then he had obviously been informed of her parentage by one of the servants.

It was early one summer's day; High Coombe was at

its very best. Nature seemed determined to compensate for the horrors of the winter. The trees were abundant in their fresh green, rooks cawing lustily from a newly restored rookery. Lush meadowsweet, poppies, cow slips, even a single late bluebell here and there adorned the high banks of the tracks along which Margaret had so painfully made her way a few months ago. Great kingcups bloomed in the water meadows which only weeks before had been entirely flooded with the great thaw. The great stone walls of High Coombe were warmed in the bright sun and bees buzzed in Margaret's herb garden and over the trim hedges of the formal alleyways. The voices of young children, servants and master echoed from the orchard where the nursery maids' excitement over a hectic Mayday not long gone added to a general air of contentment. After such a winter, everyone appreciated the coming of summer and new life. The flocks were much depleted: newly-born young animals of all kinds, calves, chicks, ducklings, foals and goslings were precious indeed with stock so low when winter finally ended. Perhaps this sense of well-being made Nicholas careless or perhaps he was already taking Margaret's passionate concern and new mellowness for granted. 'You are a funny woman, Margaret. How many other women concern themselves with their husband's bastards? She is a pretty little thing this Alice, I grant you.'

Unexpected bitterness poured out, to Margaret's later regret. 'Like Susannah, and if the poor little creatures are attractive, its all right. If she'd been born hunchback or backward, then you would not have wanted sight of her, I suppose. How many more are scattered around and what will happen to them?'

Nicholas was riled. Her barbs had gone home, as he had shown little care for his legitimate children and certainly no thought for any others. Lady Letitia's continuing childlessness appealed to him. Although he

would not admit it to himself, Nicholas eschewed
responsibility. He was already ripe for a new foray to
London or elsewhere to conquer this lady of his dreams.
The more he thought of her (and he did so frequently)
the more desirable she became.

Nicholas grew impatient with his wife's involvement
in domestic affairs. In the mornings she went about
High Coombe in housewifely attire, a simple gown and
kirtle, keys about her waist. He ignored the special
efforts that she made with her appearance later in the
day. She was as unlike the Lady Letitia in appearance as
it was possible to be. He abhorred the idea of taking her
to London; yet he was short of money, for Margaret had
made him aware of the depredations of that long hard
winter. He had heard rumours that Drake was off on a
new expedition. Joining such a venture would establish
his fortunes.

Off on this new tack, he did not answer Margaret's
jibes, but strode to the paddock. Here Margaret found
him putting the two older children astride pones.
Elizabeth was forward, tall and long-limbed for her age,
fearless with all animals. The more sensitive Kit, aware
already of his father's indifference, trembled in the
saddle and promptly fell off. White-faced but silent, he
allowed Luke to reseat him. 'He is a milk-sop, that child,'
snarled Nicholas. 'Leave him be.' It was to Luke's credit
that he persevered, whilst Elizabeth gurgled as her
father took her in front of him and rode off towards the
sea. That was the earliest of Kit's memories: his father's
fine grey horse towering over him, Lizzy laughing and
waving her arms about, and Nicholas smiling down at
her with pride.

That night Nicholas did not come to Margaret's bed
and the next morning he was away to Dartmoor to visit
his sister. It was a casual decision: Nicholas was aware of
the disasters wrought by last winter's storms and
resultant floods, but it did not occur to him that a poor

Dartmoor farm was even more vulnerable than a wealthy estate, positioned near the coast.

Nicholas was surprised to find Felicity's farmyard empty and deserted. The barn doors were off their hinges, there were signs of neglect and decay everywhere. The house showed no signs of life. The windows were obscured with cobwebs and thick dust. The thatch hung reedy and ragged Around the corner came a scrawny red-headed boy of about six years of age. His eyes and mouth were encrusted with sores, his stick-like legs barely covered with dirty rags and his feet were black. He hung back, terror on his face, when he saw the stranger. Out of the bushes crawled a bent old woman, equally thin and dirty, who also eyed the good-looking stranger with distrust.

'Can you tell me what has happened to Mistress Gray?' Nicholas shouted, his voice echoing in the empty yard.

'Nick, oh Nick, can it be you?' To her brother's horror, this filthy hag threw herself at his stirrup, hugging his leg and bursting into noisy sobs. Margaret's forethought had burdened him with food for the journey, which he spread out on the grimy kitchen table for the two starving relatives. Gradually he pieced together their story.

For Thomas Gray and his family nothing had gone right since Felicity's departure to High Coombe in the preceding September. It had begun with disease amongst his cattle and a poor summer crop. Then some kind of plague attacked both Tom and the younger children. Servants and neighbours fled in fear, leaving Felicity and the elder boy Tom to cope alone. They both survived the infection, taking it lightly; the rest of the family, including Tom Gray the elder, died. By then the winter had set in. One solitary pig, killed by Felicity in December and preserved by the intense cold, saved the two of them from starvation. No neighbours called in the early spring because, unbeknown to Felicity, they too, including the Vigus family, had succumbed to the appalling winter. Felicity grew too weak and apathetic to walk miles to the town.

Nicholas' feeling for his once-pretty sister ran deep and he left the pitiful farm with Felicity and her son astride his saddle. Somehow he got them home, where Margaret, remembering Felicity's kindness and pitying her condition, nursed mother and son back to health by the autumn.

Felicity requested to see her brother alone and so one late October afternoon they rode down towards the sea. She was no longer recognisable as the old crone of the early summer or even the plain plump matron of her first visit to High Coombe. Her golden blonde hair was whitened to ash but was an attractive cloud about a pale, well-featured face, lit up with a pair of wide green eyes. Her plump figure had been reduced to skin and bone and was now slender as a wand. Felicity was unlike Margaret in so many ways and not least in her ability to make the best of herself. Margaret's old gown of green damask was cut down together with some scraps of cream silk to make a passable copy of Margaret's new farthingale. Felicity had begged a pretty ruff from the gentle Lady Eleanor upon a visit to Bourne. Nicholas could not help remarking upon Felicity's recovery to health and good looks, noting as he did so the rough chapped hands of this one-time farmer's wife. 'Nick, Nick, you and Margaret have been so good to us. But I cannot stay.'

'But your farm is sold up and only for a few gold pieces. That will not keep you long.'

'I want that invested by you in some venture for young Tom. I have an idea, if you will help me.'

'There is plenty of room at High Coombe and Margaret gets lonely when I am away long months.'

'Nick, I like to be my own mistress. I want no charity.

Margaret is kind, but she is also strong and managing. I believe that Robert Fursdon would take me on as housekeeper. Lady Eleanor likes me and poor lady, she needs some help. Robert entertains a great deal and the lady is very poorly. I believe that I could persuade her. Will you take me and introduce me to Robert as a possible servant? I have never met him.'

Nicholas was puzzled but he was ever one for an easy life. Already, he was determined to keep young Tom on at High Coombe. He admired the young lad for his physical toughness and quick recovery. Tom followed Nicholas around in silent admiration, begging him for tales of the sea. This flattered Nicholas and contrasted with young Kit's silent sullen looks.

Margaret was hurt by Felicity's request, but secretly recognised that she and Felicity could not live in the same house. Felicity's bright new looks made Margaret feel dowdy. Margaret's confidence was already undermined by Nicholas' increasing restlessness and curt indifferent behaviour to them all.

So it was that the very next day Nicholas and Felicity rode over to Bourne, Margaret readily agreeing to Tom joining the nursery, at least for the time being.

7   *Bewitched*

In the years to come if anyone had asked Robert
Fursdon to describe his first meeting with Felicity Gray,
he would have been hard put to find more than a couple
of sentences, so overwhelmed had he been by the
experience.

When Nicholas rode in on that morning, he escorted
his sister to Lady Eleanor's room, where the lady was
resting after her sixth difficult confinement. Nicholas
was not anxious to meet the master of the house, with
Felicity in tow. He was not looking forward to his
meeting with Robert and the task which he had
undertaken on his sister's behalf. Had Felicity allowed
many days to elapse after her proposal, she would have
found her brother unwilling. She had forced his hand,
as he wanted a quiet life and he did not relish returning
home at some time in the future to two bickering
women and himself playing 'pig-in-the-middle'. He was
doubly embarrassed to meet his closest friend, for once
again Margaret had refused to sell Bourne because of
the claims of that brat, Christopher Bourne. Nicholas
had accepted his wife's strictures only because she had
promised to put a goodly part of the latest wool profits
at his disposal, profits much reduced because of last
winter's losses.

However he discovered Robert surprisingly ready to
accept his proposal for Felicity's future. Robert was
finding his wife an increasing burden and foresaw that a

housekeeper could be a useful go-between. A relative of the powerful Trenows, humble though her origins might be, could yet be a useful hostess in the power game that Robert was playing. Robert Fursdon did not suffer from those feelings of inadequacy which beset his friend and neighbour. He had approached his new Devon neighbours with enormous self-confidence and these gentlemen had accepted the offspring of Cornish folk as one of their own. But Robert's aspirations ran higher than that; he wanted to found a powerful dynasty. The acceptance must run so far that his growing family of sons could intermarry with the noblest in the land. Undoubtedly his growing fortune would help and that now was in pannaries, in tin-mining, shipbuilding, woollen cloth and farming. He was able to purchase more and more land for sheep, although he clung obstinately to the house of Bourne, despite the fact that he could purchase rather than lease other great houses. At heart he remained a seaman and wished to live in the west, close to the great ports of Exeter and Plymouth. As a member of Parliament, he represented those seafaring interests and he wanted a foothold at Court to secure a title. His most fervent wish was to see the Queen on progress to his own great house. His Plantagenet wife might be viewed with suspicion by a Tudor but she would always be respected as would her children. Meanwhile, a handsome housekeeper would attract powerful and influential men; her connections with the Carews, Trenows and Penhales, however tenuous, would not come amiss.

Robert expected some buxom farmer's wife, prematurely aged by the experiences of the last six months. He was taken aback by Felicity. Her ash-blonde looks and white complexion, in this instance, were set off with a borrowed dark green riding habit. It was in fact the one in which Nicholas had first clapped eyes on Margaret. Her manner was subdued yet spritely, her Devonian accent already overlaid again with her mother's genteel vocabulary, recalled in the weeks spent at High Coombe. She laughed at Robert's jokes, argued but not for too long over the merits of two rival sheep strains and finally revealed an elegant length of leg as she strolled into the bowling alley down in the orchard and tripped over a fallen apple bough. Nicholas was amused: he knew his half-sister – the least clumsy creature in this world. The upturned skirts were nicely hitched to one side with style and agility. So that was the way of it? Nicholas shrugged off the thought. He would be gone: the situation was not of his choosing. Felicity must fend for herself; for her, secretly, the most favourable portent was that the unholy fever which had swept off her husband and family had left her barren, or so she surmised. Nicholas noted that Felicity forbore any mention to Robert of her six-year-old son, to whom she was apparently devoted. No doubt she traded on Margaret's maternal instincts – first Alice and now Tom!

The boy was heartbroken when, within the month, he lost both mother and uncle, but there were compensations. He grew to love his Aunt Margaret, who made no distinction between him and her small son, in fact she appeared to favour him, in that she treated him as a young man upon whom she could rely. She gave him a pony of his own: she allowed him freedom to trot down to the sea, where he explored all the coves. He learnt to swim and he cajoled the fishermen into taking him to sea. In return for privileges, he took all the younger children under his wing. Elizabeth soon forgot her new-found father in the company of her jolly cousin who carried her around on his shoulders and swung her high in the air. Even Kit could not keep up his jealous resentment in the happy atmosphere which the unselfish Tom created around him. Luke was the new father whom Tom found, who told him endless stories of sea and voyaging, and he escaped to him as often as he could get away from the new tutor, employed jointly by Lady Eleanor and Margaret.

Visits to Bourne meant that Tom saw his mother from time to time. But she was now fully occupied in charge of a great household. The Lady Eleanor had been quick to relinquish responsibilities. She turned more and more to her priest and to her prayers. She spent long hours on her knees. Increasingly she occupied her time in converting her neighbours and educating her sons. For unbeknown to her blind and careless husband, Eleanor was a fervent Roman Catholic. Despite the fact that Robert was a local justice of the peace, whose duties included forcing the attendance of parishioners at church, his own wife was excused on grounds of ill-health. Her priest, an insignificant faded little man, posed as her secretary, whom people failed to notice, despite the fact that he went quietly about the county on an ancient nag, administering the Host and hearing confessions. He was a surprising person, who despite his apparent insignificance, won the respect of the three wild young Fursdons whom he secretly tutored in the Romish faith. The rest of Eleanor's sickly brood died off in infancy.

Felicity was not blind and realised that her knowledge of the Lady Eleanor's religious activities gave her a hold over her mistress, should she need to use it. But she was careful to treat Robert Fursdon's wife with the utmost courtesy and deference. She made herself indispensable to the weary aristocrat, running the household with great competence. As a farmer's wife and daughter the dairy held no fears: her butter and cheese making were of the best, so lazy dairymaids went in awe of her. Woe betide any girl who did not leave the shelves and floors spotless or who entered the great rooms in a grubby gown or apron! Felicity was obsessed with cleanliness, so the laundry too bore signs of her ever-constant vigil. In the still-room she had learnt enough from Margaret to get by, although over the years she showed an increasing interest in herbs and remedies and spent her few spare moments combing the countryside for rare plants and roots. Felicity, like Nicholas, was intelligent and she soon mastered the etiquette of rank within the household. The servants did not love her for she did not win affection as Margaret Penhale did, but they had enormous respect for her energy and constant supervision. This was when they began to suspect her of supernatural powers. It was curious how she did know everything that went on, for when Robert Fursdon was at home she was frequently at hand to meet his every wish, to fill his tankard with sack, to listen to his worries about the price of wool or the hazards of the sea-voyage of his latest ship. She was absent therefore from the kitchen, not present when the slaughtered pigs were cured or the neats' tongues prepared or the spices brought in Robert's ships sorted and stored. But if aught was wrong, she knew immediately.

Felicity's only real difficulty was in remembering to address her master in the proper tone and manner. For in bed he was her 'Robbie', a name which was wont to double him up with laughter. Robert Fursdon was resourceful, not only in the way that he had risen from lowly birth as the son of poor fisherfolk to be the suitor of a Plantagenet. His ingenuity had enabled him to uncover a hidden tunnel in a corner of Bourne which ran to one of the small chambers of the first floor up a stone staircase. He often wondered if the monks had used it for similar purposes! He came at night to Felicity's chamber and found her a ready pupil in games of love into which experienced whores of Exeter and London had introduced him as a green lad. Felicity's agility in bed, her style and elegance, her wit and diplomacy surprised him. This was an unlikely farmer's wife and daughter: then he remembered the scandalous and beautiful Lady

Elizabeth Carew, her mother.

However Robert was not given to much thought, rather to action. In these years he was well content. Felicity made no demands, graced his table, consoled his wife and ran his household with enormous efficiency. In her turn, Felicity was desperate to retain Robert's attention, so it was that she visited a well-known wise woman way over the moors towards Bovey. She planned the visit carefully, during one of Robert's many absences, and she took a saddlebag on her fine mare, realising that the journey would keep her away overnight. She confided in no-one, except her mistress, whose permission she asked to visit a relative of the Grays. She did not arrive in the hidden valley until dusk and she found her way through the gorse and blackberry bushes with considerable difficulty. To her surprise she found the wise woman to be little older than herself, deeply tanned with large dark eyes and long curly black hair. Before she opened her mouth, the woman said, 'You have come for a love potion.' Felicity was impressed, not realising that the witch had many visits from lovesick women or those desperate to drop a babe. Felicity looked prosperous, bore no sign of desperation, so the woman's words were bound to strike home. Invited into the dark recesses of a hot kitchen, for it was the end of a very warm summer's day, Felicity was fondly greeted by a collection of fine sleek cats, tabby, tortoiseshell and jet black. Their mistress turned in interest, 'Ah my fine lady, you have the gift.' Felicity was flattered. 'Yes, I can heal and I can see into hearts.'

'More than that,' the gypsy answered. 'More than that. I can help you tomorrow with a potion. But now I must depart.' She looked into Felicity's face, her eyes almost boring into her visitor's head. Slowly she said, grasping the other woman's chin, 'Why not come with me mistress?' Felicity was like her brother, always ready for excitement and new experience. So she took her companion up behind her and the mare trotted obediently up the valley. There was now a moon overhead and the moors were drenched in moonlight, every fern, every gorse bush clear and quivering in the odd radiance. Felicity wondered then and later what was real and what imagined. High on the moors the women gathered, young girls and old crones, who, soon after their arrival, began to dance to the eerie note of a single shepherd's pipe. In and out, they wove their way around the great boulders, and in the centre was positioned a large towering rock, flat on top. After some minutes, making Felicity from her observation post jump with fright, a dark, horned figure sprang up on this flat surface, capering, jumping and beckoning. One young girl let out a shriek and leapt, almost flying, into the arms of the creature. They stood together, coupling, the horned one thrusting himself again and again, the girl's head thrown back in ecstasy. Felicity found herself wet with perspiration. The other women had thrown off their garments and danced white in the moonlight. Felicity felt her nipples harden, her groin wet. She felt possessed; excitement rose in her, as it did when Robert would come at her from behind and lift her on his manhood. She felt herself tremble and float. Recklessly she threw off her gown, her petticoats; she joined the throng, and danced till she fell, exhausted, on the young heather. She slept.

The next morning she found her horse cropping nearby, in the early sunlight; only the birds sang and a few sheep called to each other, no other sound penetrated. There was no evidence at all of the events of last night. Slowly she found her way back to the wise woman who looked older, wrinkled and grey in the sunlight: she had a vial in her hands. All she said was, 'I shall see you again soon.'

The coven drew Felicity back again and again, even in the early winter when the frost sent her limbs tingling.

But the heat remained and one night he beckoned her and they rose high above the moors: she seemed to be floating in his arms. This time he laid her flat, thrusting again and again fiercely and wantonly she arched her back in response. Now the servants began to murmur, seeing her increasing absence. Noting her pallor and the dark rings under her eyes, her mistress asked her if all was well. Felicity has ceased to ask permission for her nights away and the lady made no comment. Her housekeeper was too valued and she knew that Felicity's silence regarding her own secret activities was secured by her Penhale connections. She would not bring the world crashing about the ears of her brother's best friend. Robert remained in ignorance of the pursuits of the two women, one with God and one with the Devil.

* * *

Margaret knew nothing of this. She was taken up with a further pregnancy, easier this time. Nicholas had ridden off to Court, but she knew that he would come back to High Coombe some time. She was reconciled now to the pattern of her life with him. He would never stay long: he would take the money, as he was entitled to. But one day he would return with a fortune, high in the Queen's favour. The Lady Eleanor's life was the same, but it was worse for her because she was always sick. Margaret was well enough to hunt, to visit neighbours, to supervise the estate, to enjoy the companionship of her children. When John was born in September 1577 she was content. In that year Nicholas sent word that he had joined Drake's expedition.

Nicholas was himself in despair. Discreetly, he had courted the Lady Letitia, now returned to London. Recklessly, he purchased jewels and conceits to present to her: he found himself one among many. In the midst of a fantasy, he failed to perceive her overwhelming greed. The sight of her tall, elegant, slim figure, leaping in a galliard, sent him into a paroxysm of passion. He could not control it and daily grew more short-tempered. To his horror, he let slip a careless remark about the forty-one-year-old Queen's declining attractions. He lost the few friends whom he had so carefully acquired. Nothing mattered except this dark beauty. When her elderly husband died, the suitors were thick as flies. He was in despair and would have sacrificed everything for his wife to fall downstairs as the wife of the Queen's favourite had so conveniently done.

During these waiting months he had two trysts with his lady – one in the gardens of Hampton Court on a glorious summer evening when the Queen's musicians provided a faint echo of great occasion. The next was far less judicious – in the lady's barge, when she was far less conscious of the watermen than he. To her, servants did not exist and, on this one occasion, he was able to take her perfumed body close to himself, to bury his face in her white bosom, to kiss the full red mouth. Next day her betrothal to one of the country's wealthiest men was announced. In despair, he threw himself upon Sir Francis Drake's mercy and signed on for the Indies. He sent a message to Letitia, begging her to meet him close by his lodgings. There was no reply. On his last night at Court he heard the strains of lute and dulcimer, which had haunted the moonlight garden at Hampton Court. Sunk in self-pity, he felt that his life was over. The message to Margaret read: 'God knows if I will return. It is a perilous undertaking for Queen and country. You and the children must take pride in this great service to which I pledge myself.'

In her ignorance, Margaret did not see the overwhelming vanity and egotism. Prayers were said in the village church for them all and prayers for safe-keeping from the hands of those devils, the Roman Catholics.

Lady Eleanor heard these words when Robert escorted Margaret to Bourne for a great feast with neighbours. She sat at Robert's right hand and Margaret sat at his left. Felicity was commanded by the Lady Eleanor to oversee the procession of dishes carried into the hall with great ceremony. This time she was aware of the waves of jealousy which overwhelmed her as she stood at the back of the chamber close to the archway, through which the servants walked in solemn order up to the high table. Felicity's fine ash-gold hair was hidden under a dark cap; although her gown was of deep green velvet, it was simple and her fine bosom was hidden by a white kerchief. Not once did Robert glance her way; only the retainers were aware of Felicity's fierce looks and darting, venomous glances, which went always in Margaret's direction. For Margaret had dispelled the gloom engendered by news of Nicholas' departure and sat laughing at Robert's jokes and talking in a most animated fashion to her other neighbour. Once she threw out both her hands in a generous lively gesture and smiled at Felicity as she did so. Margaret remained unaware of the hatred which Felicity's whole rigid body seemed to express, so quickly was the object of this discharge caught up in the good fellowship of friends and neighbours around her.

Felicity retired to the kitchen to scold the servants and to insist on the scrubbing and polishing, which went on past midnight. 'She's a devil, that one,' they murmured to one another, behind Felicity's straight back. At long last Felicity stood naked in the moonlight in her own bedchamber, where Robert found her and took her in a fumbling, drunken fashion, which she totally ignored.

Far away Nicholas sailed out on the wintry seas of 1577, supremely unaware of the threat to his wife and family. They were to have no news of him for three years.

PART THREE 1581–1582

8   The Sailor's Return

As Nicholas rode down through the valley of the Exe in the late spring of 1581, it was much as it had been on his return from voyage in 1572. The countryside still glowed in the warm sunlight, lush green meadows and dark dappled woodlands, sparkling streams where the trout leapt, banks of mingled wild-flowers, scented meadowsweet, abundant birdsong. Yet Nicholas was almost unrecognisable. It had been a terrible voyage, harder and crueller than even he, the experienced sailor that he was, could have expected. Enormous stormy seas, hostile natives, and always the dangers of uncharted waters. Would he ever forget the hazards of the Spice Islands? He would wake at night in a sweat at fears of the rack and thumbscrew – the dreaded Inquisition – it was as though he felt the burning fires prepared for the bodies of heretics. Yet Nicholas had never believed himself a coward.

His sandy hair was sparse, his beard grizzled, his tanned face deeply lined. His melancholy seemed an unlikely reaction, for they had arrived in Plymouth in the previous September to a heroes' welcome. Drake had brought back an immense fortune in ducats, which Nicholas accompanied to London, where it was stowed in the Tower. Drake commissioned a great crown of diamonds and emeralds for the Queen and she wore it on New Years' Day 1581. Nicholas shared in the surge of patriotism which overwhelmed the Court.

At Court, Lady Letitia had been kind, for Nicholas was one of the heroes of the hour. Drake was the people's great idol. However Nicholas surprised himself: he found the dallying about Court tedious. He was wealthy; he was famous. He found it turning to ashes in his mouth. He put it down to a persistent rumbling in the guts, a lethargy, which to the one-time village champion was hitherto unknown. Letitia continued to play the flirt and tease. There were tiny lines around the great blue eyes. the skin was drier and the white powder more obvious. The small white kitten's teeth were yellowing and showing signs of decay. The elaborate gowns and hosts of jewels somehow emphasised the loss of first youth. Like the Queen, Letitia never admitted to her years, which were in fact three and thirty.

Yet Nicholas could not give up the chase. In despair, he resorted to bribery, for despite the latest husband's great wealth, Letitia was as greedy as ever. She accepted his gifts but did not grant the ultimate favour. She persuaded her compliant spouse to purchase new estates at Yealmpton near Plymouth. She left for the west in early spring, as soon as the roads were passable.

Unable, for the sake of appearances, to travel with her, Nicholas took berth on a small ship bound for Plymouth. It was a rough voyage and Nicholas' condition worsened. He lay in his bunk, writhing with pain for much of the voyage.

So it was that he rode homewards in the early spring of 1581. It was on impulse. He had promised Letitia to attend her at Yealmpton as soon as possible. But let the minx sweat for once! Perhaps he had been too eager. Draw off a bit and let the hunted become the huntress. It was a technique which he had employed so successfully with others. Nicholas did not admit to himself that he was dog-tired, that he needed the peace of High Coombe. He was actually looking forward to

Margaret's steady care and cosseting. He was even curious about his children. Was the young Elizabeth growing into a beauty? What of the new baby?

Unknown as yet to his father, John had been born on September 7th, the Queen's birthday, in 1577. For the first time Margaret had time to give her full attention to one of her offspring. She fed him herself. He was like Elizabeth as a baby, fat, chuckling, content. The young Elizabeth had grown into a petulant, stormy little girl, quite unlike her brothers and half-sister. She showed every sign of beauty, with her mother's colouring but the fine features of the Carews. But she was not attractive – she seemed to dislike her mother. In her father's absence she became spiteful with servants and animals. Jealous of the attention John received, she got steadily worse. Indeed behind her mother's back the servants called her a 'spoiled brat'.

In August 1580, when her father was sailing towards Plymouth, she and her brothers and her half-sister were playing by the stream beyond the paddock. There had been a storm the previous night and the stream was unusually full. The nursery maids were careless, absorbed in making a great daisy-chain with which they proposed to adorn Luke who, despite his ugliness, was a great favourite – a real joker and tease. Seven-year-old Kit was building a dam with his friend Francis Fursdon; Timothy and Alice were tagging along behind them as usual. Elizabeth was strolling petulantly along the bank. She disliked the water, for it mussed her hair and her general appearance, of which she was always inordinately proud. She could bear no spot of mud or blemish on any of her gowns. The three-year-old John had wandered downstream and was picking kingcups for his mother. Elizabeth could just see him through the branches of a willow. She noted that her brother was tottering on the brink and heard a faint cry as he toppled, face down, into the water. She walked very

slowly towards him. That silly baby. He was always
wanting attention. She was roused from her thoughts by
the hysterical screams of a nursery maid, who had come
upstream to find her charge in the water. Tom Gray,
working in the nearby bowls alley, heard her cries and
rushed down the orchard to put the young child on his
stomach and attempt to dispel the water from his lungs.
It was too late. Typically, it was Tom, now a sturdy
eight-year-old, who ran ahead to break the news to his
aunt and adopted mother.

* * *

The lack of news was interspersed only with rumours of
complete loss at sea, yet Margaret had soon become
reconciled to Nicholas' absence. She was happier than
she had been since those ecstatic early months of
marriage. Robert and Eleanor were her companions.
She continued to hunt with Robert; they entertained
their mutual friends at Bourne and High Coombe.

Margaret was drawn into a new and absorbing
interest. Her kind heart had led her to befriend
refugees from The Netherlands and, learning of their
skills, she had built a row of weavers' cottages in a
nearby village. The charitable gesture grew into a
business. Robert too invested his wool purchases in the
weaving of English cloth.

It was an absorbing occupation for them both.

Margaret had grown into a shrewd business woman,
thanks largely to the tutoring of Robert Fursdon. A
good estate manager, she grew richer from the
proceeds of her sheep and horses. Nicholas' presence in
London and at Court, his participation in the Queen's
progress to Kenilworth with a string of mares and
geldings, had drawn attention to the High Coombe
strain. Margaret met many orders for horses of all kinds
during Nicholas' absence in the Indies. She had fine

stallions at stud and she refused to put them to mares unless they too were top quality. She began to invest these profits into trade out at Topsham and Plymouth. Her ships, the *Thomas*, the *Timothy*, the *Christopher*, were lucky, avoiding the depredations of Spanish privateers and running into port with cargoes of wines, spices, silks and dried fish. She was engaged in a most profitable trade with the Baltic as a member of the newly founded Muscovy Company. Her fleet of merchant ships grew: now she expanded into shipbuilding. Margaret purchased a house near the quay in Topsham, appointing reliable clerks recommended by Robert. But her own training at his hands enabled her to supervise accounts and control overseas factors. Her knowledge of languages was valuable. She took risks and there were some losses, but her wealth built up year by year. Kit liked to attend her at Topsham and spend hours on the Strand there watching the loading and unloading of many ships. He had an aptitude for figures and the clerks were patient with him as he did his sums. But Margaret felt that she never knew him, although she loved him deeply. One never knew what Kit was thinking.

In her paroxysms of grief at John's drowning, Margaret was aware of Kit's further withdrawn behaviour. Shyly he would kiss her hands and hug her tightly round the legs, 'Mama, Mama, I am here. I am here.' And then he wasn't, for he had hidden himself away in some far corner of barn or stable to nurse his own desperate sorrow. For Kit loved deeply – all of them. Rachel, Luke, Tom and most of all Tim, John and Alice. There was one exception; he reserved his feelings about Elizabeth. Some dim memory of a man on a white horse obtruded always on his visions of Elizabeth. Anyway he heartily disliked her screams and tantrums: he was a private little boy and was embarrassed by public display of any kind.

Margaret blamed herself for John's death. On this particular day she had been away up at Franscombe, supervising the closing of the farmhouse after Mrs Trelawney's death. The lands were absorbed by a neighbouring tenant farmer. But, illogically, she also blamed Elizabeth. Any good sister looked after her little brothers, didn't she? Margaret remembered how she had caught Elizabeth pinching little Timothy, who was always thin and ailing. A terrible thought sprang to life, but she dismissed it immediately. Yet somewhere it remained at the back of her mind. Elizabeth was to display great jealousy in the future and this fuelled her mother's terrible suspicions.

When Nicholas arrived in early May, Margaret was still reeling from this disaster. Her business efficiency and her careful supervision of her household had both been seriously impaired. She was not ready for the shock of her husband. News had filtered through of Drake's arrival in Plymouth and the great fortunes made. But all who had returned were anxious to visit London, to establish their fortunes and to make themselves known to the Queen and other persons of influence. A message from Nicholas that he would return home soon had given Margaret news of his safety. Therefore she was not surprised to see him, but rather horrified by his appearance. He looked twenty years older than the Nicholas of 1577. He seemed to have shrunk, and indeed in bed that night Margaret was aware of the wasted muscles and of bones protruding through the dry skin. He groaned in his sleep and fled too often to the stool in the neighbouring stool-house for her to be unaware of his declining health.

Wiser and more discreet now than in years gone by, she made no comment. A great hero must be a hero to his wife and no less of a man. She prayed that the rather enfeebled mounting of the night before would produce no more children. Rachel must be consulted, for preventative measures, as well as for a cure for her master's flux.

Margaret herself was knowledgeable about herbal concoctions and country cures. Within a few months, Nicholas was more his old self.

The great celebrations at High Coombe to mark his return contributed to his new optimism and vigour. Here was indeed a new master, lavish in his rewards to old servants and friends. Nicholas was proud to purchase from Margaret a magnificent black stallion with some fine accoutrements, to present to his friend Robert Fursdon for his protection and care of Margaret during Nicholas' absence.

Lady Eleanor, pregnancies behind her, emerged from seclusion to attend the feast and to receive a fine diamond. Margaret herself wore emeralds, her husband's gift. With a determined effort, she put away all thoughts of John and appeared at her most attractive, gowned in orange (her favourite colour) and dark green, with a beautiful lace ruff, imported from The Netherlands by one of her own factors. Her curly hair was dressed by one of the refugees, trained in the household of a French nobleman. Margaret was scarcely recognisable to herself in the mirror which Nicholas had presented to her on his arrival.

Felicity, who had been called upon to attend the Lady Eleanor, was appalled. Who could have believed that the dowdy Margaret would become so attractive in her later years, winning the attention of so many men present at this great gathering, arranged to welcome Nicholas home? Felicity remained in the background but she watched them all, Robert, Eleanor, Margaret, Elizabeth, Nicholas and Letitia. Her meetings with the coven seemed to have given her new powers and in the bright sunshine she seemed to see great shadows over them all. Or was it just a cloud over the sun?

Neighbours had come from far and wide and were to

be accommodated at Bourne and High Coombe. The Lady Eleanor had escorted Lady Letitia Lowe and had introduced her to Nicholas and Margaret; the lady was at her most affable, congratulating Margaret on the setting of her great house. 'Infinitely more attractive than the Abbey at Yealmpton. We have plans to rebuild, haven't we, Hugh?'

Hugh, who had married Letitia for her fortune rather than her figure, was admiring Margaret's plump contours and her emeralds. The Trenows, like the Fursdons, were 'parvenues' but Letitia seemed set on cultivating the county, so the gallant Hugh bowed low over Margaret's white hand. 'Madam, I am honoured. As my wife remarked: High Coombe is a fine estate. It would give me great pleasure if you would escort me on a tour round the garden.'

Letitia, who was a silly woman as well as a flirt, smiled coyly at Nicholas over the head of Lady Eleanor. Nicholas was taken aback, as he had never imagined his wife and his beloved meeting. Reluctantly he took Letitia's arm and they strolled up and down the terrace. He whispered, 'Why have you come? You are not welcome.'

'La! Nicholas, do not be so ungallant. I expected you to be very pleased. You are always saying that you wish to see more of me. I had no idea that you were so wealthy, or should I say that your wife had a fortune?' In fact she was well aware of Nicholas' circumstances but she was an everlasting tease.

With great hauteur Nicholas rose to the bait, 'My dear lady, my voyages with Drake have enriched me beyond your wildest dreams.' Hastily he drew a large ruby from his doublet, one he had intended to present to Margaret. He could not resist a public demonstration of his new wealth.

From the back of the terrace the Lady Eleanor had marked their progess, the two heads, sandy and dark, close together. She saw them stop and Nicholas hand something over with a bow and flourish. She sighed on her friend's behalf. Robert had come up behind her and with a light tap on the shoulder, 'What are you observing so closely and with such a frown?' She turned away, saying lightly, 'Some folly of Nicholas'.' Robert laughed, well aware of his wife's dislike of his friend; it worried him not at all.

Meanwhile, Letitia took the ruby, examining it most closely and tucking it down between those two delicious peaks which dimpled above her square-cut gown of heavy crimson brocade, the nipples just out of sight. She found herself observed by the most charming child, clad in a gossamer gown of aquamarine which reflected her sea-green eyes and contrasted with a mop of deep russet curls. The little girl curtseyed slowly, turning to Nicholas, 'Papa, you should introduce us.' Letitia observed the pride in Nicholas as, gravely, he brought forward his daughter, and she murmured, 'What a beauty. She will set hearts aflutter in a few years.' Then she began to talk to the small girl, who was completely won over by being treated in such an adult manner, actually being consulted on her opinion of the gowns around her. She pouted, 'I told Mama that hers was too elaborate and stupid.'

'The Queen wears just such a gown,' said Letitia, tactful for once.

'But she is the Queen.'

Quickly Nicholas butted in, 'But your mother is a queen around here. Now run off and find Christopher. Where is the boy?'

Elizabeth was forever Letitia's slave when she said, 'Sir, I have seen your lovely daughter. I need no more than that. Come, Elizabeth, or may I call you Bess? I can tell you about our great monarch after whom you are named. Walk with us.'

'Have you seen her too?' said Elizabeth, skipping along in great excitement.

Her father was reconciled to her presence. She could well save him further embarrassment.

'You shall play for us on the virginals,' he said.

'So she is musical too,' exclaimed Letitia, in delighted tones. She found herself taking to his poppet who looked up at her with such adoring eyes. 'Not only must you play, but you can ride over and visit me at Yealmpton.'

'You can see my pony, "Hobgoblin",' said Elizabeth with pride. 'He is the very best in the county. No hedge is too high for him.'

Whilst his daughter chattered on, a plan was forming in Nicholas' mind. Why not adopt an old-fashioned custom and allow Elizabeth to join the Lady Letitia's household? There would be endless excuses to visit the Abbey and his lady-love.

The reverie was interrupted by the three of them coming face to face with Robert Fursdon. He swept Elizabeth off her feet, lifting her high into the air above his giant frame. 'Put me down. Put me down, sir.' The guests around were amused and entranced by the sight of the little girl's antics, surrounded as she was with the three handsome figures of their new county neighbour, Lady Letitia, and of Nicholas and his friend.

Coming up with them, Sir Hugh and his companion were unnoticed. Margaret was irritated. Why must Elizabeth always be the centre of attention? Where was her handsome Kit?

Far away in the stable, young Kit cuddled a wolf-hound puppy, presented by his friend Robert. Straw was sticking out of his new purple doublet and white ruff. He would have to return, for portraits were to be painted. But nobody was missing him. Luke was busy with preparation and serving. Even the extra servants could not cope with the mounds of food prepared for house and courtyard, where tenants would eat. Kit's eyes filled with tears. His father had brought him nothing: it was the thoughtful Robert who had filled the gap with the pup. It was the first thing of his very own, apart from the ponies and they couldn't be smuggled up to his turret room. How lucky that Mama had moved him to the furthest end of the house, close to Luke, but away from the other children, even Tom. But Tom had gone all silly, following Nicholas around and gazing up at him. Tom had forgotten Luke and his stories. He wanted to know all about Nicholas' ship the *Pelican* – every detail. Well he, Kit, would not be a sailor; he would be a fine merchant like Robert, have a beautiful house on the Strand, full of great grey wold-hounds.

So Luke found him sound asleep on the straw, his arms around 'Rowley', the dog, and Luke carried him quietly to bed. The sounds of revelry did not penetrate to the back of the house. Indeed a lone buzzard called to its mate and that was all to disturb the peace on the moorside. Nicholas and Letitia walked sedately along the alleys of Margaret's garden. Her tinkling laughter could be heard away on the terrace where Robert escorted his wife and their hostess. 'This was indeed genius, Margaret. A fantastic success. I am so pleased that you invited the Lowes, Eleanor. They are old family and a great asset to the neighbourhood. In addition, like so many of us, he opposes the Queen's marriage to Alençon. He sees the danger that the Queen is in from the new Jesuit mission. Campion has been racked.'

Lady Eleanor stiffened. 'Please Robert, no talk of politics on this glorious day. The Lord Lowe is over there, looking slightly bored, why not join him and talk your tedious parliamentary affairs to your heart's content?'

As Robert moved away, Margaret would have dearly liked to join them. But loyalty to the ageing Eleanor held her. She was more and more aware of the powder keg of Eleanor's religious fanaticism. Robert was a devoted member of Parliament, a justice of the peace;

should he learn of Eleanor's double treachery to the Queen and to him, Bourne would be torn apart. Margaret shivered as the twilight deepened. Trust Nicholas to find the most attractive woman present and to lure her away.

'How you have changed, Margaret. No jealousy now.'

Thoughtfully Margaret said, 'Nicholas cultivates old families, people of influence; for him the ladies are easy game.' Complacently, she thought to herself that Lady Letitia was a little worn at the edges; for herself, Margaret had been flattered by Lord Lowe's attentions and the warmth of admiration in Robert's eyes. Lightly she turned the subject to her sister-in-law. 'Why did Mistress Felicity slip away so soon?'

Lady Eleanor hesitated. 'These days she keeps away from company. I am not sure what is happening.' This was not strictly true, for the intelligent older woman had soon become aware of her husband's liaison with his housekeeper. But, free at last of Robert's physical attentions, Lady Eleanor was at liberty, especially at night, to cultivate her religion. Now neighbouring Catholics attended secret mass and only last month a Jesuit had arrived and was even now hidden in a secret cavity behind the chimney-piece of Lady Eleanor's private parlour. With Felicity's implicit connivance, Lady Eleanor had appointed more and more indoor servants of her own religious persuasion. Even her sons' new tutor was a scion of an old Catholic family. Tom Gray, Kit and Timothy kept the old tutor busy at High Coombe. Francis Fursdon, aged eleven, was growing into a serious young man, devoted to his mother. The secrecy of their religious education had turned the wild little boys into quiet and orderly youths, the pride of their boisterous father, who gloried in their scholarship. No scholar himself, Robert could yet appreciate learning and foresaw great opportunities for the new dynasty, founded on his wealth.

As twilight deepened, the Fursdons, Lowes and other guests who lived close by or who were staying overnight at Bourne, departed. Nicholas and Margaret played host to house-guests.

The travelling artist had been observing them all day and had asked if he might paint some portraits on the morrow, to mark this great occasion.

Nicholas himself carried the screaming Elizabeth to bed, calming her with a promise that he would take her on a visit to her new friend the Lady Letitia. He had a deep and abiding love for his daughter. Her volatile personality was like his own and he was the one who could calm her after one of her screaming tempers. He could join in her laughter and fun when she was getting her own way and things went well. She, in her turn, was very demonstrative, putting her arms round his neck to squeeze him tight. Sitting on his lap and petting his face with her soft white hands, tickling his beard with the mass of her red curls. He was proud of her beauty and her dignity on public occasions. By contrast, he had no love or understanding of his son: he found his beauty effeminate and his interests alien. Nicholas preferred the physical challenge of life at sea or difficult fences in the hunt. He liked to wrestle with his servants or school his horses. Unlike his neighbour, Robert Fursdon, he had no respect for scholarship and took no pride in Kit's prowess in the schoolroom or his obsession with figures. He did not seek him out to talk about ships because Kit showed no interest in sailing before the mast but rather in the design and the trim of his mother's sailing ships. Continually bruised by his father's neglect and scorn, the boy drew further and further into himself, silent at meals, creeping away as quickly as he could to escape to his room or to the moors with his beloved 'Rowley'. Kit had few friends but those he made were sure of his sturdy loyalty and deep affection, amongst them the studious Francis Fursdon. Together they would pore over the books in Bourne's famous library and together they would study the habits of woodland and river creatures, deer, foxes, badgers, otters and owls amongst them.

Both lads sought to escape their fathers. Kit found his parent rough and crude, ill-mannered towards his mother and over-familiar with the servants. Francis lived in perpetual fear that he would betray his religion and thus his mother to his father. So although Robert admired and respected his son and sought continually to draw close to him, Francis grew more and more reserved and silent. He was his invalid mother's constant companion and support, totally sharing her deep religious convictions. Poor Kit had no such solace. He was frightened of betraying his very real hatred of Nicholas to his mother who was so obviously devoted to his father and would never hear ill of him. So Francis' friendship was doubly precious to him, along with that of his dog and his pony.

All this was far from Nicholas' mind when he left Elizabeth's chamber and joined his wife in a new mood of optimism and elation after the great day. He took her tenderly. It was a Nicholas Margaret had not seen since their early courtship. He was solicitous of her passion, stroking all her body, her breasts and loins, till she cried out for him. Even then as he thrust, he held back until, looking into those soulful brown eyes, so full of tears and love, he drove on to a height they had never reached before. Afterwards she lay in his arms and heard the nightingale.

Next morning Margaret rose early and leaving the sleeping Nicholas watched the sun rise over the sea through the Foxhole Gap. It was a moment of beauty that sustained her through the following months of a difficult pregnancy.

As for Nicholas, he continued to treat her with great kindness. He seemed settled and happy. She noticed his frequent visits to Yealmpton where Elizabeth was now living in Letitia's household. In her heart, Margaret was glad to be rid of the girl's tempestuous presence; guilt assailed her, but Nicholas assured her that Elizabeth was happy, and that Letitia could prepare her for a brilliant future at Court. Margaret hoped that Nicholas would begin to take more notice of his other children, especially Kit. In later years, with great sorrow, she was to realise that in Kit's most desperate need not only did Nicholas fail him but so did she.

9 *Treachery*

It was true that Felicity and her mistress had, without words, entered into a contract. Eleanor ignored Robert's essaying into Felicity's bed and Felicity the growing Catholicism of the entire household, she and Robert only excepted. For, despite all attempts by Eleanor, Felicity resisted conversion. She was not a religious person anyway; if she worshipped at all, it was the Devil.

As Robert's visits fell into less exciting and more predictable patterns, so Felicity's obsession with the coven grew. She was aware that the grooms found her black mare sweating and blown on many an early morning. But Felicity's hissed warnings of retribution went home: the lads were young and reared to fear the Devil and all his works.

Felicity had to ride hard over the moors to the chosen spot, disrobing with speed to join the frenzied dancing ending with a magnificent coupling with the horned and hoofed black creature, atop the sacred boulder. Felicity lived for the moment when she was the chosen one. The creature too craved her, large, ungainly, unrecognisable in any human form, he wanted this tiny slender creature of dynamic force. She rose in sheer excitement and hysteria to unparalleled heights, especially on those wild nights of wind and storm. The brilliant light of a full moon provided further thrills, the silence broken only by the echoing cacophony of the owls' song, birds who haunted the woodlands at night. By the side of this, Robert's play degenerated into a pale shadow of former passion. Robert knew it and kept Felicity for those moments of frustration which seemed to come less frequently as he grew older.

Felicity suited him: she ran the place with enormous precision: she and Eleanor were friends. There came a time when he ceased to use the tunnel; it seemed to coincide with Nicholas' return.

His old friend would invite him over to Yealmpton Abbey, which always seemed full of guests whether Sir Hugh Lowe was present or not. But Robert came to dislike Letitia; he found her continual flirtatiousness irritating, her tinkling laughter silly and her conversation frivolous and tedious. He could not help contrasting her with Margaret and wondered at his friend's folly. For Nicholas, along with his own daughter, seemed to hang upon every word which his mistress uttered. He brought over a stream of expensive gifts – jewels, horses and fine silks. Robert knew that Margaret was pregnant again and he recognised from his experience with Eleanor that a husband's role was frustrating. But he himself missed Margaret's company and did not understand Nicholas' constant visits to Letitia. One evening at Yealmpton when he was trying to hide his yawns in the company of Letitia and her friends, the lady drew him on one side. With a silly giggle, she said, 'You have a wonderful opportunity to visit your mistress.'

'But the Lady Eleanor is away on a prolonged visit to relatives.'

'Not your wife, sir,' said Letitia scornfully, 'your mistress!'

Robert flushed, thinking that she referred to Felicity. Yet no-one knew of that affair or so he thought.

Seeing his hesitation, Letitia went on, 'Whilst Nicholas is here, Margaret would surely welcome your presence.'

'Margaret?' Robert's tone was puzzled. 'Margaret?'

Yet on the way back the following day, his thoughts revolved around that seed, sown by a foolish woman. In all these years Robert had only seen Margaret as a true companion, one whose interest matched his own – politics, trade, shipping, hunting, falcons. Now he saw her in his mind's eye, not beautiful but serene and handsome, large bosomed and, unlike his wife and mistress, warm and comfortable. It seemed almost blasphemous to imagine her in bed, but this is what he began to do. Why had he not seen it? He was in love with this glorious creature.

When, in mid-October, Margaret failed to go full-term and gave birth to a still-born daughter, it was Robert who, defying convention, rode over from Bourne to enter her chamber to take her gently in his arms, to let her weep inconsolably, and who finally let her go, kissing her gently on each cheek. He stayed whilst she slept – old Rachel slumbering in the corner, the old crone's thought, 'At last. At last.'

When Margaret awoke next morning the body of the dead infant had disappeared and Margaret felt surprisingly peaceful. Her tears had been for John, for Nicholas, for fading hopes and disappointed expectations, for the long lost years. She gave no thought to Robert. She scarcely remembered his presence on the previous day. She slept again, on and off, for several days. On the third day there arrived on a golden cushion a delicate single pearl, no message. Margaret did not need to ask from whence it came. Richard Bourne, long years in his grave, might smile that Bourne had brought him his revenge on Nicholas Trenow. To Margaret, the pearl was the symbol of a love, which, for long years, she and Robert had hidden not only from the world but from themselves.

Only a few miles away across the valley, Bourne lay in confusion.

After his visit to Margaret, Robert had ridden off to Plymouth. He was thinking of his love, her eyes large in a face thin and white with the anguish of a childbirth. He failed to notice a group of gentlemen coming into Bourne from the opposite direction. It was a bright clear day, but their bobbing heads only appeared between the trees from time to time. Robert himself was well on his way by the time they pulled up their sweating horses before the front of the great house.

Unceremoniously, they dismounted, hammering on the great oaken door, calling, 'Open in the name of the Queen.' Frightened servants ran out from stable and barn. But still no-one came to throw wide the entrance passage which led to the Great Hall.

One of the gentlemen, a corpulent red-faced creature in dark doublet and hose and great thigh-length boots, ran forward to drag a pimply youth who gawped at him from the stable door. 'Fetch me your master or your mistress. We are on the Queen's business.'

From round the corner of the drive, out of the woodlands a small figure emerged. Gravely courteous, Francis Fursdon enquired, 'And what, sir, might that be?'

The corpulent gentleman's companion thrust the lad aside, almost knocking him to the ground. But Francis remained smiling and courteous. 'I am the master in my father's absence. Francis Fursdon at your service.'

'Well, young Master Fursdon. Fetch us your mother at the double or we shall cut down the door.'

Francis said slowly, 'My mother is sick and cannot leave her chamber. Tell me your business or call again when my father returns from Plymouth.'

'Insolent brat, open the door or...'

Francis interrupted; in a cold clear, high voice. 'My mother, sire, is a relative of our Queen and my father a member of Parliament and a justice of the peace. How dare you?'

'We dare you, sire, we dare you,' was the rejoinder. 'The Queen's life is in jeopardy and we have information that a Jesuit lies in hiding here.'

Francis paled, but drawing himself up, said very slowly, 'You are at liberty to search. Jeffard, open the door.' Slowly, the great door creaked open.

Unceremoniously, the five men burst in, down the long stone passage into the Great Hall where Robert's great mastiffs stood guard under the eyes of Francis' brothers.

'Call them off or by God we'll draw our swords.'

The young Paul Fursdon quavered, 'Yes, yes sir,' and obedient as always, the mastiffs sat growling softly in their throats as the unwanted visitors poured out into kitchen, buttery, parlour. Francis then heard the clamour of their boots and voices as they mounted the stone staircase to his mother's chamber. He ran up the backstairs, white-faced; he stopped before the open door of the room, where his mother sat before the great fire, hands in lap, serenely facing her inquisitors. Together, they heard other members of the party hacking at the panelling, crashing open chests and cupboards. No-one spoke.

The fat red-faced man said finally, 'We have found nothing. But be sure, Madam, we will. This house will be watched. We have reason to believe that you are a Papist in league with that scarlet woman, Mary Queen of Scots.'

Then and only then did the Lady Eleanor reply, haughtily and crisply. 'Sir, my husband will hear of this. And it is you who must watch out. There is no more loyal subject and friend of the Queen than he.'

'Madam, it is you who are reported, you who are of treacherous Plantagenet stock.' Here he stopped and spat a long stream into the heart of the fire where a great log had just taken light. Mesmerised, Eleanor and her son followed its course.

Back down the stairs thundered the five men in their boots and spurs, shouting to the frightened servants for their horses.

Within a minute, Francis was pulling out the flaming log, stamping out the flames; smoke filled the chamber; Francis pulled a great stone from behind the firedog. Lady Eleanor hitched up her skirts and called for a bucket of water; Francis' hands were burnt, his face scorched, smoke made him cough violently; he never forgot those sensations when, in later years, in foreign and distant lands, he saw and heard the shrieks of heretics in the great 'autos de fé'.

Eventually, and with great difficulty, they dragged from the stone, coffin-like opening the long lean body of the Jesuit. All attempts at revival were of nought: he had suffocated from the fumes which filled the opening. How many times Lady Eleanor had discussed with her sons and their retainers the safety of this priest hole. Whilst Francis had dallied with their Puritan enemies before the house, the Jesuit had crawled frantically into the hiding-place whilst a great fire was built up and thrust back against the stone.

Never strong, Eleanor was exhausted by her efforts, worn out with the strain of wondering how long Francis could delay the intruders whilst the Jesuit father was hidden. Now she wept and her sorrowing children and servants put her to bed; on her instructions, they carried the Jesuit to the chapel where he lay on a low wooden table before the altar. Rare and expensive candles burned. Eleanor's wizened old priest, garbed in embroidered vestments, knelt in prayer, keeping watch through the night. Francis tried to point out the dangers to his mother, but she was too weary to think.

The household slept. Out of the night came a great thundering on the door. This time there were no plans; the boys slept away in the west wing; the servants were too frightened to resist. The mastiffs sprang up in great joy to meet their returning master.

Robert Fursdon was fearsome in his great rage. En route to Plymouth, he had heard of the raid by Puritan neighbours, justices themselves, jealous of Fursdon fame and fortune. Robert rampaged up the stairs and into his wife's chamber where she sat, white-faced and shaking. Robert sought to commiserate with her. 'I will have them imprisoned and fined. I will make them wish they had never been born.' Eleanor's little maid had come on the scene, barely fifteen and new to the household. 'Oh sir. Oh sir, we were so afeared that they would discover all.' Suddenly there was a heavy silence. Eleanor shivered.

Francis and his brothers had been roused by the frightened major-domo and rushed into their mother's bedchamber to stand before their father, interposing their bodies between him and the Lady Eleanor.

'Leave us. Leave us,' he spat. 'You deceiving whoresons, you brats, you swine. She is safe. You are not.' To Eleanor he said, 'Madam,' as coldly as he had spoken with heat the moment before, 'you will be confined by me in that great dungeon at Buckingham. I might have known that the blood of Edward of York and that whore his wife Elizabeth Woodville could bring forth no issue but that in the style of Richard Hunchback.' Robert's long resentment of his high-born wife was vented at last. 'Madam, you have betrayed me. I have honoured and respected you. You have dragged me through the mire. Far, far worse you have raised our sons in that vile religious persuasion which threatens our country. The fires at Smithfield, lit in Mary's time, smoulder still. The stench remains in the nostrils of all good Englishmen.'

He turned on his heel and rode off towards High Coombe.

For an hour the Lady Eleanor sat paralysed. No servant came. No sound disturbed the heavy blackness of the great house. With an effort Eleanor rose and with enormous haste, after descending the great staircase, she gave orders to the servants, who cowered together in one corner of the Great Hall. She summoned her children to her.

When her husband returned next morning, Eleanor met him at the door. His sons were gone, despatched to Douai, lost to him. The Lady Eleanor lived, if that is what it can be called. Imprisonment at Buckingham was described as that for a demented soul. Madness ran in the veins of those with Neville blood, so no-one challenged Robert's orders. The Catholic servants from Bourne had long since fled. Felicity was nowhere to be found.

Robert was never to see Felicity again; he heard that she had taken shelter in the farmhouse at Franscombe where she lived with her cats, increasingly eccentric, feared by her neighbours. Nicholas made no attempt to see her. When Margaret sent messengers to her, they were driven off.

Half-demented, Felicity laughed and laughed. For she had intercepted that messenger who carried the solitary pearl to Margaret. Felicity no longer wanted Robert for herself, but she would not surrender him to that plain sister-in-law whom she had despised and envied for so long. For years she had seen Margaret take her place at Robert's right hand, she had seen them laughing and joking, talking about trade, Parliament, the Queen; subjects about which she Felicity knew nothing. She could not join the chase or sit down at the feasts. She had to attend to the servants, the household. The early experience of the Dartmoor farm had begun a process of unhinging her brain. The ecstasies, dangers and mysteries of the coven added to it.

She was deeply hurt by Nicholas' neglect, he who had not visited her since his return from sea. Young Tom Gray was Nicholas' man. It was all Margaret's doing, so she would destroy her.

Robert had ridden to Margaret for solace. In her new-found love for him, she was unguarded. 'I have feared this for years. The times are hard. I knew these Catholic neighbours would talk and it would come to the ears of the Puritans.'

Robert stopped in his pacings up and down her bedchamber. 'You knew. You knew. You did not warn me. You were aware of the dangers; you understood the consequences for me. I will never ever forgive you.'

Margaret could not believe her ears. She was to blame. For her loyalty to Eleanor, her belief in truth and justice, for not coming between husband and wife. Was this her reward? As Robert left, she flung herself from her bed and, but for Rachel's restraining hands, she would have thrown herself from the window to the terrace below.

A fever set in and when Nicholas returned, recalled by the faithful Luke, he found Margaret delirious. Riding over to Bourne, he found the great pile silent and deserted. It was some weeks before he put together the whole story. Even then, there were two pieces missing from the puzzle. Margaret's love for Robert remained hidden behind her closed face and stony eyes. Felicity's treachery to everyone at Bourne in sending a message to the Puritan Justices was to remain a secret for years to come.

No-one gave a thought to Kit, who crept around the house white-faced as any ghost. Devoted to his mother, he had been close to her chamber during her difficult confinement. He had heard her shrieks, had smelt warm blood, and had hated his father more than ever. Then he had observed Robert's messenger and gift and the new sparkle that had come into his mother's eyes. So when Robert arrived that day and stormed into her presence, Kit had rejoiced at the implications for his father. But he overheard the conversation which grew louder and louder. Friendly as he was with Francis, he was unaware of the boy's religious faith but, fearing for him now, he rode post-haste to Bourne to find the place deserted. The whole place was locked, shuttered and barred. A few riding horses champed in the stables, the pigeons and doves cooed from the loft. No other sound penetrated that courtyard which only last week had echoed to the sound of many servants, of domestic animals and the general bustle of a great household. Kit was in despair, but so strong was his faith in Francis that he awaited some message. It was some years before he understood that his friend would not endanger another family with the taint of Rome in any form.

Kit wept inconsolably; only Luke tried to rouse him from his torpor. Margaret remained locked in her own grief. As always, Kit evaded his father on the few occasions when he was present.

PART FOUR 1586–1594

Elizabeth

10 The Invitation

In the four long years since 1582, Nicholas had not been back to sea. He had grown corpulent and bloated, having spent many weeks in the year dallying after the Lady Letitia. She sulked when her new husband went north to Scotland on the Queen's business and in a fit of pique sent a hasty message to bring Nicholas over. He could not believe his luck, for when he arrived the house was quiet. He stabled his own horse, the servants absent or in their quarters. He had long resented the feverish activity of the small court gathered around Letitia. Had it not been for the frigidity of his wife and the frustration of a defeat, he could have foresworn his worship.

Since the still-born birth of her daughter, Margaret had withdrawn more and more into herself. She refused utterly to share his bed; she had lost all interest in the estates, even the breeding of horses. However, she became utterly absorbed in trade and shipbuilding, spending more and more time down at Topsham. Their fortune grew.

Young Kit was her shadow: he took over the weaving, dyeing and finishing business. Robert had sold his share in this to her.

Since Drake's expedition in 1577, Nicholas had plenty of gold, and High Coombe had little to offer. He was concerned only with one of his children, Elizabeth, and she remained at Yealmpton Abbey, growing into a precocious, sulky beauty. Despite her emotional tantrums, Elizabeth was an intelligent and talented girl and yet she modelled herself upon the empty-headed beauty who was her constant companion. But Elizabeth had always been jealous of her mother; she had begrudged even the short time which her parents spent together. Aware of her own beauty, she scorned her mother's homely appearance. She was deeply resentful of the fact that Margaret blamed her for the drowning. She was aware of her father's infatuation with Letitia and encouraged it, delighted when her parents became increasingly estranged. She was not so pleased when Letitia banished her to Exeter on this particular occasion, when the lady finally decided to summon her love. Perhaps she at last recognised that here was the real rival for her father's affections.

It was to be short-lived, for Nicholas had waited too long. Letitia had prepared herself most carefully for him, determined to submit to his passion at last. She bathed in asses' milk, she washed out her eyes with belladonna to make them sparkle. She brushed her long dark hair till it shone, plucking carefully any grey intruder. Her tiny breasts and flat stomach were not marred in childbearing; she had seen to that. She even painted her nipples. Her hands were small, her legs long and ankles neat. All this she admired in her new and expensive mirror.

Nicholas was taken aback to find the Abbey empty and echoing, for it had always seemed so over-full of chattering and excited guests, interspersed with hurrying servants, anxious to please an exacting mistress. Letitia was dressed in a loose flowing gown of dark red burgundy, a colour which was always becoming to her. She took her lover by the hand into her darkened bedchamber. Wax candles burnt in one corner, where a large bowl of dried pot-pourri gave forth a pleasing but pungent odour. Long practised in the arts of the bedchamber, Nicholas found Letitia's moves forced and artificial. He recalled the subtlety of the French courtesans whom he had known. He was thrown off balance by the unexpectedness of his mistress' surrender. He had always preferred the chase to the kill anyway. Letitia herself found the coupling curiously unsatisfactory. Lord Lowe was now dead and Letitia's fourth husband, Richard Glisson, though plain in looks, was more vigorous than the handsome but ageing Nicholas. Courtesy prevented either from speaking their thoughts, but Nicholas rose from the bed, announcing his early departure to Exeter to fetch Elizabeth. Letitia was irritated; she had adored the child but she was now growing up and Richard Glisson was a little too interested in her protégée. Languidly, she said, 'Perhaps it would be as well to take Elizabeth back on a protracted visit to High Coombe. She misses her mother.' Both were aware that this was a blatant falsehood but Nicholas was pleased, as he had no desire to visit Yealmpton more than he need. It was Letitia's final stupidity to take Nicholas to her bed, when a continuing frustration of his desire would have kept him faithful for ever.

It was with relief that he rode down through the streets of Exeter to Robert's town lodgings. He found his twelve-year-old daughter sitting on Robert's lap, tweaking his beard, and Nicholas' first reaction was one of jealousy, but Elizabeth jumped down to greet him ecstatically, covering his bearded face with kisses. He and Robert laughed at the antics of the pretty creature, finely gowned in light green brocade and a daffodil yellow farthingale, her chestnut curls bobbing, as she leapt a galliard with an invisible partner. She was a fine dancer and a good musician too, entertaining them on the virginals and singing.

'By God, I'll take you to London. That is what I'll do.'

'Oh Papa, Papa, I do love you. Shall Robert come too?'

Nicholas noted the use of the Christian name. 'You
had better call me Nicholas, minx, if Robert has that
privilege.' Sending word to Margaret, Nicholas rode off
with the pair of them within the week.

Robert had important Parliamentary business
anyway, as London was agog yet again with news of the
suspected treason of Mary Queen of Scots. They all
lodged together at Nicholas' old lodgings in Cheapside
where he had installed an ex-mistress, now happily
married, to keep a comfortable home for him. She
fussed over them all and especially Elizabeth. She cooed
over the girl's wardrobe, which Nicholas had ordered
Letitia to send. He was horrified to learn that Letitia
had brought the dresses to London in person. But she
kept away from Nicholas; he was not to know that she
was busy experimenting with love-philtres and beauty
potions, with an old crone on nearby London Bridge.

Nicholas was enjoying the company of his vivacious
daughter too much to care about Letitia. Elizabeth
explored the City with him, laughing at the antics of the
'conies' in St. Paul's yard and the gallants strolling with
assumed modesty, but high ostentation, down the
centre of the crowded noisy streets. Hammers were
beating in one place, tubs hooping in another, water
tankards running at a tilt in the third. Merchants
harried their clients. Money bags clinked; porters
sweated. When Elizabeth saw the great houses with their
landing-stages on the river, she begged her father to
build or buy one and set her up in charge. 'A
twelve-year-old child, I ask you,' Nicholas told Robert,
laughingly.

But it gave Robert an idea and soon he was taking
Elizabeth to look at sites, talking to architects and
making elaborate plans. Nicholas was jealous and
decided that he would take her to the Blackfriars
Theatre where a new actor, William Shakespeare, had
just arrived. The play was full of blood and thunder,

great cracks echoing forth from behind the balcony, bodies covered in blood left on the lower stage to walk away at the end. A ghoulish figure rose up through one of the many trapdoors to send a shiver through the audience. Elizabeth was entranced and talked of nothing else for days. These happy months of 1586 were drawing to a close, for Nicholas ran into John Hawkins at one of the taverns; they fell into serious talk about the Spanish menace. So Nicholas decided to escort his daughter back to High Coombe, before paying a call on his old captain, Francis Drake.

Elizabeth was bereft, but she got little sympathy from Robert, who, unbeknown to her, had been summoned urgently back to Buckingham to his dying wife. Hoping for news of or indeed sight of his sons, he decided to set out post-haste. He promised Elizabeth that she should come and stay in the great house which he was building on a site chosen by them both and planned on leisurely afternoons by the three of them.

Margaret was delighted to see her daughter back, after an absence of three years. In June 1587 Elizabeth celebrated her thirteenth birthday, in her father's absence. As Elizabeth had been away for so long, Margaret made a great occasion of it, like the old days, with feasting and dancing. Kit acted the host. Grave and mature beyond his fourteen years, he was very slender, with delicate features and bright chestnut hair. He was handsomely dressed, like any court gallant, in white hose, a fine doublet of black and white, jewelled gloves, a sparkling ruff and a scarlet feathered cap. Timothy by contrast, twelve years of age, looked younger, a pale, colourless little boy whose fine dark blue outfit seemed to swamp him. His shadow, the petite Alice, was the fairylike creature she always had been, with brilliant blue eyes and pale ash-blonde hair. They stood quietly on the terrace behind their mother, talking to each other, almost oblivious to the lively gossip and chatter of neighbours and friends who came to greet their sister. None of the children liked Elizabeth; she was still spiteful and selfish. She teased children, dogs and horses; Kit suspected her of being downright cruel. But he kept the peace, for his mother's sake. He tried to keep an eye on Elizabeth, as he believed her to be capable of any deceit. He knew that she sent messages to London; since he thought that they were to the Lady Letitia, he said nothing. He was well aware of his father's infatuation; his mother was not. Soon after Elizabeth's arrival, he threatened her with loss of fortune if she told her mother the truth. Elizabeth was well aware of Kit's hold over her mother and of the great Penhale fortune. She knew that her father had won wealth in the Indies but she saw him spending it recklessly, and feared for her own future.

On this glorious June day, Elizabeth chose to forget all that. She had allowed herself to be robed in a gown of shimmering white overlaid with pearls. Her stomacher of palest peach set off her creamy skin and chestnut colouring. All the county decided that she was destined to be a great beauty. On this occasion, because she was the centre of attention, the mouth ceased to pout and her heavy-lidded eyes were sparkling green. Suddenly she left her mother's side and bounded across the terrace and round the corner, throwing herself into Robert's arms. It was fortunate that the crowds were busy and they were hidden by a jutting turret. 'Steady, mistress, steady.' Robert bowed low, his eyes full of admiration. 'Oh Robert, you came, you came. Isn't this the most glorious day?'

From behind his back, he drew a beautiful silver ring, chased and adorned with tiny pearls. 'Oh Robert, I do love you. It is beautiful.' As she went to kiss him once again, he drew back. 'Elizabeth, you are no longer a child but a beautiful woman. You must behave with more circumspection.'

She belied his words for, like a child, she laughed and stepped away.

At that moment her mother came round the corner and stopped, pale-faced, on seeing Robert. He bowed low, hiding his dismay that Margaret had changed so much. The gentle serene creature of his dreams was so hard-faced, so stern, so withdrawn.

'Madam, I received your invitation and could not decline to join this happy family party.'

'Invitation?' Then Margaret bit her lip, looking at the conspiratorial expression on her daughter's face. As Elizabeth had calculated, Margaret would not lose her dignity publicly by disclaiming all knowledge of such an invitation. For, by now, friends had gathered round to greet the ever popular master of Bourne. Gossip was hard at work, for his sudden disappearance, together with wife and family, had given rise to much conjecture.

Now that the meeting with Margaret was over, he was his old gregarious self. Like Nicholas, he had put on weight; however it was not a corpulence but an overall bulk which made him seem an even more masterful giant. He was full of humour, danced with as many women as possible, young and old. He apologised to Margaret for his past behaviour and told her that he was opening up Bourne and that he sought the old friendship. As for Margaret, she reserved judgement, but she was driven to Robert's defence by Kit's increasing anger and resentment.

'Kit, he is your father's greatest friend and mine. I don't understand; you and he were once friends.'

'Tim does not like him either. He's not to be trusted. He's like some old fox. What has he come back for? Is London too hot to hold him? He should be helping prepare against the Spanish invasion.'

Even when Kit learnt that Robert's contribution was a well-equipped ship to be captained by his own father on his return, he remained suspicious.

He had long reconciled himself to the loss of his friend, Francis Fursdon. But his misery had turned itself into resentment against the father. How dare he neglect his family to the extent that they could turn Catholic without his knowledge? How dare he laugh and joke on this sunny morning when his sons were irrevocably lost to him? He saw the growing friendship of Elizabeth and Robert. It was now Elizabeth who insisted on hunting with Robert, who presented him with falcons and even found him a falconer and other servants.

Margaret was distraught. One minute she was thinking what a fine match it would be for Elizabeth and an advantage for a Trenow to be linked to a great mercantile fortune. The next moment Margaret was aware of her own feeling for Robert. He continued to be affable and kind, including Margaret in the chase and when she was so inclined, talking over business with her.

One evening at High Coombe, she questioned him about Mary Queen of Scots, and the Queen's peculiar behaviour; they talked of The Netherlands and the Queen's desire to avoid war. The young Elizabeth did not take kindly to being ignored, so withdrew, haughtily, to bed. Then Robert spoke of Eleanor's death, how she had forgiven him and he her. His sons had not come; there was too much danger, especially at Buckingham, where Eleanor's family leanings towards Rome were known. Times were dangerous.

'But I have no heirs,' said Robert. 'Francis is studying at Douai to be a Jesuit priest, but I learnt recently that both his brothers are dead of the plague. At least Eleanor was spared that loss.'

'Oh, Robert. I am so sorry.' Margaret's barriers were down. She was once again the kindly creature whom he remembered. As he wept, she cradled his head in her arms. He kissed her gently when it was all over. He looked into her warm brown eyes and recognised Margaret of old.

It was Margaret's turn to confess how wrong things were between Nicholas and herself. She obviously knew nothing of Letitia; he did not enlighten her. But he did realise how Nicholas' tempestuous nature, with its temper tantrums and inexplicable silences, had worn her down, along with her pregnancies. For the first time for many years they felt at peace with each other. This peace was soon to be shattered by the force of great events.

11   Great Events

When Nicholas arrived home from the expedition to
Cadiz, Margaret was seriously alarmed. More than ever
he was short of breath. His high colour came and went.
Despite the vicissitudes of the voyage, he was fatter. He
was thirty-four years of age and looked an old man.

Secretly, Margaret tried to persuade Robert to
withdraw his offer of the captaincy, but Robert pointed
out to her that Nicholas would be offended beyond
endurance. All the neighbours knew of the command.
Nicholas talked of nothing else. But he spent his four
days at home, learning more of his other children. He
regretted that he had always kept Kit at a distance. He
saw so much of the Carew heritage in him; he was a true
gentleman, old beyond his years, astute and far-sighted
in business. This time Nicholas was interested in the
family fortunes, in the effect that the impending war
would have on the wool trade. He was pleased to see
how Kit had diversified his activities. There were plenty
of merchant ships, an interest in minerals, a new
investment in Exeter silversmiths. Nicholas was proud
of his eldest son, but he found it difficult to get near the
boy; unwittingly, a quick call at Yealmpton on his way
up from Plymouth had set Kit against him. Nicholas' call
was unlike him, for it arose from remorse as well as
nostalgia. The lady, widowed once again, was from
home. Had she known it, she had worked her revenge.
Nicholas' stop-over at Yealmpton further estranged him

from the son whom he was just getting to know and to admire.

Arriving home, Elizabeth demanded Nicholas' attention but he found her vivacity and restlessness too much in his present fatigued state. This annoyed her and so she teased her father by absenting herself at Bourne. Like Margaret, Nicholas foresaw a great alliance. Robert had no son other than a Catholic heir and must marry soon. Before he left, Nicholas spoke gravely to his daughter. 'Please learn from me. Treasure what you have. Do not always be looking beyond the rainbow. You are beautiful and talented; you shall have a great dowry. Be content.' Elizabeth turned away with a sullen smile. Nicholas caught his breath, suddenly his mother sprang to mind, the same pouting, kittenish beauty was revealed. 'I shall enjoy my life. Don't worry. I shall have what I want.'

'What is that, darling?' replied her father. But the entrance of Tim and Alice prevented her from replying.

If Nicholas was at a loss with Kit, with Tim it was far worse. The boy seldom spoke: he was obviously in fear of his great burly father. He knew that his father despised his diminutive size, especially his poor performance on horseback. He had great prowess in the dairy – understood butter and cheese-making, enjoyed the breeding of good milk-yielders. If Nicholas knew of these things he discounted them as girlish. So it was that Timothy was entirely ignored in the will that Nicholas drew up in Exeter in 1588 on his way to join his ship. At Margaret's request, he bestowed a sizeable dowry on Alice.

Both Margaret and Nicholas were aware that this parting might be their last. This attempt against the mightiest power in Europe was a hazardous one. The air was full of rumours about the great galleons of Spain and the vast army of men which they accompanied. This new voyage might tip the balance of his precarious health. On that last night, within the privacy of their great bed, they turned to each other. Margaret rested her head on his great chest and said, 'Do you remember our first night in this very room?'

'I shall never forget it, sweeting. You were so warm, so welcoming and full of gaiety. Oh Margaret, what have I done to you over the years? I have not been a good husband.'

'Hush, darling. I would not have it otherwise. Oh Nicholas, Nicholas, how I have loved you.'

Neither of them noticed her use of the past tense. Neither looked for the passionate heights of previous reunions in that great bed, but instead Nicholas took her with great tenderness, softly kissing away the tears rolling down her cheeks. 'Hush, hush, my love. We will have a new start. We will beget another brood of fine children. This time I shall stay here and rear the finest horses in the country.'

Sadly Margaret did not believe him. But she closed his mouth with a warm kiss. The perfume of lavender and gilly water swept over him and he nestled in against her back and slept. She lay awake, listening to the owls calling to each other. Wasn't that a good omen? In the breeze, Diana bowed her head and drew back the bow.

Nicholas had taken a number of men from the surrounding countryside, with sea-going experience. But he insisted on leaving a goodly force, to whom he had given some elementary training. The great fiery beacon on the hill behind the house would give warning of the Spanish approach. High Coombe would be defended; he left Tom Gray in charge. Both men were heartbroken, for his nephew had given him stalwart service. He was a plain-featured, sturdy young man of sixteen, but he had seen service on land and sea. He was level-headed, cool in any crisis. He and Kit were friends. Nicholas was not aware that the only reason he was persuaded to stay was Elizabeth. Tom had always loved her; unlike the others he ignored her faults, charmed by her waywardness, adoring her beauty and vivacity. He made no attempt to ingratiate himself. Perhaps, for that reason, she did not taunt him, altho' she suspected his passion. On a particular morning in July he forbade her to ride to Bourne, pointing out that all the signs were that the Spanish were on their way. Rumours were already rife of the Spanish sailing in May.

Terrible storms had rent the whole country. The deep claps of thunder, the jagged lightning, the dark in the midst of day, seemed to portend the end of the world. The young Elizabeth had ridden time and time again through heavy rain to join Robert in entertaining guests or in riding down to Exeter. She had her groom but no other chaperone. Daily she expected Robert to declare himself; that he failed to do so with Nicholas had not however surprised her. She knew her father's jealous nature and that Robert was older than her own father.

For Elizabeth was besotted with the older man. Her deeply sensuous nature responded to his overwhelming masculinity, for Robert Fursdon exuded virility. His giant stature was allied to his dark saturnine looks. His luxuriant black hair and beard was matched by black hairs which curled over his chest and even on the backs of his hands. The sight of them could rouse Elizabeth to a pitch of pleasurable expectation. As a young child she had sat on his lap and now, to his simultaneous embarrassment and gratification, she sought again and again to repeat the gesture. Robert was grateful for his cod-piece which masked the mounting and over-whelming desire. She is only an infant, he would tell himself, and my lover's daughter to boot. And indeed this was part of Elizabeth's charm that she was half-woman, half-child. She had a curvaceous and enchanting figure, a pretty face and the kittenish, petulant manners of a spoilt minx. Robert enjoyed her

company for half a day but he could not have borne her
demands and her tantrums for much longer.

On this particular morning in late June Elizabeth
rode slowly through the woods towards Bourne; she
had bribed her groom to leave her alone in much the
same way as her mother had sent Will away on the
fateful day of her mating with Elizabeth's father.

It was early May and the trees were bright with that
burnished green which so soon fades with summer suns.
A mist of bluebells carpeted the ground and the whole
countryside rang out with the sound of mating birds.
Elizabeth was humming a tune, unbeknown to her one
composed by Henry VIII during courtship of Anne
Boleyn; she was lazily switching the overhanging
branches with her crop. Indeed her arm was raised, as
round the bend of a slight incline rode Robert,
handsomely and flamboyantly attired in a brilliant
scarlet doublet and hose. A black feathered cap was set
jauntily on his head, from which he removed it to bow
with exaggerated courtesy over his horse's head.

'Well met by sunlight,' he quoted. It was not lost on
her for she had been privileged to visit the theatre with
Robert and Nicholas.

'La, sir,' she rejoined in a flirtatious tone. 'I had
thought you had forgotten me.'

'Never will that day come,' said Robert, matching her
wit with his own. 'You are far too beautiful ever to be
forgotten. You must remain in any man's memory as a
vision of youth and loveliness.'

Elizabeth pouted and pulled her horse. 'I am more
than a vision, Robert. I am a woman.'

Her companion too had reined in his horse and now
they confronted each other. 'Come, lass, you are no
more than a babe in arms.'

Coquettishly, Elizabeth slid from the saddle. 'I am not
in your arms however.'

Looking down at that lovely face, framed in thick

russet hair, glowing with health, eyes sparkling and wide scarlet mouth curled upwards in a smile, Robert's heart melted. He felt the throbbing in his groin, his limbs turning to water. He stayed in the saddle, gripping the leathers tight to prevent himself succumbing to an overwhelming temptation.

Elizabeth turned away, gathering in her arms great garlands of bluebells and ferns. Laughing, she said, 'Bend down, you great creature, and let me crown you Oberon to my Titania.'

As she stretched up to encompass his neck, his eyes caught the shape of her breasts, over which her riding-habit was stretched. The nipples showed hard and pointed through the silken velvet. He extended a hand and she arched her body against his fingers. She licked her lips, the smile gone, the face full of anticipation.

With a great bound, Robert was out of the saddle. 'Elizabeth,' he groaned. 'Elizabeth.' Now she caught both his hands in her own, dragging him over to a grassy mound. The horses were forgotten and wandered off through the glade, harness jingling. Birds flew frightened out of the thicket: the harsh call of a predatory jay added discord to the cacophony of birdsong.

Robert and Elizabeth were oblivious. She drew him down, touching his bushy eyebrows and beard softly and with awe. 'What a great hairy creature you are.' Tenderly she unloosed his points, rubbing her hands over his chest. 'For so very long I have wanted to feel that great mat,' she said, drawing in a deep breath.

Now Robert was roused beyond thought, beyond decency and beyond reason. He was tearing at her clothes, first to touch those enticing breasts. No Venus ever had such a delicious contrast of pink and white. The belly was taut, the legs white alabaster and slender, encasing his manhood, so that he thrust again and again. Now she screamed and he started to withdraw, but her legs were behind his back and she gave out little cries of ecstasy, which drove him mad. Never had he known a woman more passionate, with a more intuitive skill for arousal.

After a long time, they lay entwined in each other's arms and the smell of bruised fern was all around them. Lazily she said, 'Robert, I love you.' She was so satiated with passion, so innocent in her responses, that she failed to notice his abrupt tone, which he sought to soften. 'Come, chuck, you will be missed. Without a chaperone, too.' Here he laughed. 'Oh, Elizabeth, you'll be the death of me sometime.' So they rode back, separately. He was so shaken by the experience that he resolved never to be alone with her again. And it was this resolution which drove Elizabeth crazy with frustration: she was never one to be thwarted in desire or resolution.

Elizabeth was so enthralled with Robert's passionate lovemaking that nothing could keep her from him. But, with the news of the Spaniards' approach, they had all conspired against her and locked her in the room. She did not see the beacon flaring, but she was aware of people riding in from far and wide. She was allowed to come down when Robert himself arrived. Her mother was busy preparing food for servants, tenants and visitors. Messengers came in from the coast with news of the great ships passing far out at sea. Winds had kept them out of Plymouth. Elizabeth was genuinely concerned for her father and shared her worries with his friend. 'This is his finest hour. He has never before captained a ship. He is with the Queen's own force which will defeat the enemy. Make no mistake, the Spanish are not experienced at sea. Keep them away from The Netherlands where they hope to collect a great force of soldiers. Then we shall win.' Robert's words were proved right. The fireships at Gravelines, the great storms which drove the galleons on to the rocky shores of northern Scotland and Ireland were the allies of Hawkins, Drake and their sailors, men like Nicholas.

Nicholas' return was awaited. Preparations were in hand for great celebration. This time Robert planned one from Exeter, so that it would be part of a great city ceremony of friends, beginning with a service in the cathedral. It could no longer be delayed for Nicholas' return, so Margaret, Elizabeth, Kit, Timothy and Alice found themselves in a front pew of the great cathedral. Outside, the crowds in the cathedral yard jostled to catch a glimpse of the great men of the day. Robert strode in, accompanied by his merchant friends of the City Council. Afterwards there was an enormous ox roasted down by the harbour, where two small ships, which had taken part in the fighting were moored. The Trenow family stayed overnight at Robert's lodgings and next morning set off in bright sunshine for High Coombe. Impatient as always, Elizabeth rode ahead; fronting the crest of the hill she saw a slow procession wending its way into the courtyard. Fear gripped her: she could not face what she would find. 'Please God Thou has delivered us from a great evil. Deliver us this day.' She turned her horse into the woods; it was typical of her that she hid the truth from herself for as long as possible. Before Margaret Penhale came into the archway, she knew what she had tried to avoid thinking of in the past weeks. Nicholas was dead – not in the battle, in which he had proved himself such a great captain, but of a fever which carried off so many sailors from the force which had set off from Plymouth on that summer's day.

Although Margaret had expected it, she was still stunned. Somehow the lack of news about her husband and the great rejoicings in Exeter had allayed her fears. She mourned Nicholas, the bright hopeful ambitious boy she had married. She forgot the lonely years, the years of neglect. She remembered the sunny days amongst the horses in that first year of marriage. Kit and Tom took charge. It was a great funeral. Hundreds of people came to pay respect, not to the individual but to the event. It was a sorrow but it was also a triumph.

When Margaret rode back to High Coombe, scorning the uncomfortable carriage, Robert Fursdon was by her side. Kit felt so neglected that he took himself off to Topsham and thus missed the visit of the lawyer. The estates were divided; Bourne and the mercantile business and houses in Exeter and Topsham to Kit; the rest to Margaret without reserve, except for sizeable dowries for both girls. To High Coombe was added the fortune which Nicholas had won on his voyage round the world.

To Elizabeth's surprise, little of her father's fortune had been dissipated. But she was disappointed. She was pleased that Kit had not got High Coombe – no-one knew that Kit was Nicholas' son but Elizabeth knew that the pair hated each other. However, Elizabeth had believed that High Coombe would be hers. She had remembered his last words and took it to mean that she should be content with the fortune that he would leave to her. She shrugged it off; Robert was rich. He needed an heir and she believed herself to be pregnant.

Old Rachel, her mother's nurse, was long dead. Elizabeth had no-one in the house whom she could consult, until she heard Tom Gray mention that he had visited his mother who was skilled in the healing arts.

Two weeks after her father's death, Elizabeth rode to Franscombe to consult her. She sent the groom over to Bourne and rode alone. Her mood was mixed; she missed her father, although she had been separated from him by long absences. But the last two or three years had drawn them closer together; both moody they had quarrelled, but both found these quarrels and reconciliations exciting. But Elizabeth felt exalted and yet at the same time apprehensive about her pregnancy. It would be a boy, Nicholas Carew Fursdon. Robert would be so pleased and she would persuade him to live in London. They would go to Court and Robert would be knighted. She would see to that. As she day-dreamed her way up the track she failed to notice the heavy silence, the lack of birdsong and the oppressive heat.

Elizabeth became aware of it as she turned into the deserted and overgrown farmyard. About half a dozen cats screeched out of the stable as she locked up her horse. Turning, she saw a young blonde woman come to the door, then she saw that the blonde hair was white and the features blurred, almost debauched. Elizabeth shivered.

Felicity's West Country accent was back. She greeted her niece. 'My dear, you are my mother's double. For sure you are. What a proud beauty.' And then as a suspicious afterthought, 'Has *your* mother sent you?'

'She doesn't know I've come. You do know that father is dead?'

'Yes, God rest his soul. Tom visited me. He's a good lad and usually comes when he is home from the sea.'

'Oh, Tom.' Elizabeth had almost forgotten the relationship, since she regarded Tom as one of her father's many servants.

Inside the farm kitchen it was very hot; a great fire roared in the grate but it was clean and well-kept. Elizabeth had heard rumours of witchcraft here, but there was no evidence, except a huge ginger tom-cat that rubbed itself against her legs. She was given a hot brew and some bread before she was able to bring the conversation round to the subject of her choice.

Felicity smiled to herself. She guessed what was coming. For Felicity knew all about Elizabeth from Tom. Tom, who said so little about anything else, was loquacious about his young mistress. Felicity had long since forsaken her jealousy where Tom was concerned.

He visited her and kept her supplied with flour and other food. In her eyes he was perfect, partly because he recalled the halcyon days of her innocence with Thomas Gray her husband. Her son was staunch and faithful in the same way and he loved this maid.

Felicity had continued to attend the coven, as a grave elder to be consulted. Occasionally she was called to service her master, the Devil. Her real interests now lay in travelling around the surrounding countryside, where her skill with herbs and potions put her in considerable demand. Tom kept the pony supplied, so she rode in some style. But she lived in complete isolation and gossip about her was rife. Her career was so astounding that people did not understand her – a farmer's wife, a gentleman's mistress, a lonely forsaken crone. There were stories told in dark chimney corners about Robert and Lady Eleanor. Poor lady. What had happened to her? It was Felicity who was held responsible. Nicholas Carew's restlessness was also to be featured in her – she went from one role to the next, each one a new challenge and a new interest. She had loved Robert, but she had scorned his weakness in falling victim to her plot. She had respected the Lady Eleanor and would have liked Robert to be a staunch husband in adversity. She despised him for throwing off his own family so easily. Her considerable sexual energies were now largely redirected into the mysteries of healing. Her character was so contradictory as to be inexplicable. Yet it was simply that she was very passionate but her passions flowed through only one channel at a time.

Felicity surveyed the beautiful young maid with some interest. Of High Coombe she knew only what Tom chose to tell her, so when Elizabeth confessed to her pregnancy, Felicity assumed that it was Tom's doing. She examined the girl, pronounced her healthy and in need of nothing but a husband. Elizabeth flushed and hesitatingly asked for a love philtre. 'Why my love, he's so keen already that he's given you a babe.' Elizabeth did not want to reveal Robert's name, so she was careful. 'Yes – yes – but I want to keep him that way.' What she really wanted was to sweep Robert into marriage, but she could hardly say so. Understanding the whims and fancies of a pregnant woman, Felicity gave her a harmless concoction of rosehip and rosemary and they parted friends, albeit in ignorance of each other's thoughts.

12 Revelations

Margaret was a person who had always been honest with herself. It had begun on that dreadful day when she had discovered Nicholas on the bed with Susannah and she had fled across the hills to Bourne. The Lady Eleanor had helped her to face the truth about her husband and thus about her own position. Now there was no-one to whom she might turn. Kit was barely sixteen years of age, already immersed in the responsibilities of the commercial and financial empire centred in Topsham and Exeter. It was astounding that one so young could take on so much responsibility. It was sad that Nicholas Trenow had just begun to appreciate his son's sterling qualities when he was called away once again to serve the Queen, never to return. Anyway Margaret could scarcely say to Kit, 'Nicholas Trenow has been in his grave barely four weeks and I am shaken with love and desire for another man.'

On this particular morning with the mists of early autumn coming close about the windows and around the russet glory of the trees beyond the garden, Margaret felt that the swirling mists were like her own emotions. Every now and then a shaft of sunlight penetrated, revealing blue skies above the gloomy grey shroud which covered the woods and moors. She felt guilt spinning in her mind, making her body heavy and weary, then suddenly she would flush with the memory of Robert's tall, virile figure, his splendid dark head, set upon his wide shoulders, the firm full thighs in their fine doublet and the bulging calves rippling in the silken hose. Above all, she remembered the dark ardour of his black eyes, flashing mischief and humour. She had so many affectionate memories – of the chase on the cliffs above the sea, of her skirts entangled in gorse as she raced Robert on the hills high above the estuary, of banter at high table, secret jokes between themselves. She could feel his warm red lips on her hand as he bowed low before her, ever one to treat her as a great lady. She could feel the very slight pressure on her rings as his strong muscular hands clasped hers, gently but subtly. Even during the weeks following Nicholas' funeral, when he would visit to help her with the multitude of business arrangements about wool and weaving, arrangements which they shared, he continued to touch her with such delicacy that he conveyed devotion and, at the same time, a hidden ardour. She remembered his single pearl on a velvet cushion, sent in at the time of the birth of her last child. She shivered in remembrance of that last pregnancy and the repeated desertion of Nicholas at all times of sickness and trouble. For so many years Robert Fursdon had been close by, to console and to strengthen her by his very presence.

Margaret felt that she should be in mourning for Nicholas, but her regrets had been in years past, for the sturdy, healthy lad who had ridden around the estate, broken in the horses, managed the beloved stallions, who had become the ageing man, who was plagued with fever and bile and who strove to pretend that he was still the fiery lover of her youth. She was saddened by Nicholas' refusal to face the truth, that he was no longer young and that the girls, whom he still pursued so relentlessly, laughed at him behind his back. He might represent power and wealth, the successful courtier whom the Queen welcomed, the sailor with his tales of storms at sea and privation on far distant shores, but in his own person the exact opposite of his neighbour and friend Robert, who seemed to retain an air of youth and optimism, despite increasing girth and a sprinkling of grey hairs in his springing curls and beard. No. Margaret could not mourn. She could be overwhelmed with pity for a man who had pursued his dreams in vain, who had never known that he was seeking perhaps a woman who had died long years ago, who for Nicholas stood for ever at a farmhouse door, gazing, with clouded eyes, westward towards her childhood home. Margaret shook herself impatiently. Perhaps she was wrong, perhaps Nicholas had enjoyed the taste of success; the achievement of a personal fortune, the recognition of his monarch, whom he worshipped from afar. Resting by the window, looking down across the gap towards the coast, where the mists had dispersed sufficiently for her to see a faint sparkle of light on the sea, Margaret was shaken from her reveries by the entry of her maid, who waited hesitantly in the doorway, sensing her mistress's mood.

Indeed Margaret started when the maid announced, 'Robert Fursdon,' as if her guilty thoughts had been read, as if she was already naked before this man, whom she so ardently desired. She descended the great staircase slowly, her eyes to the ground. She wore a plain gown of dark brown, adorned only with an orange kerchief; her keys were at her waist and her cream petticoats swung beneath the heavy overskirt. Her thick hair was hidden beneath her simple cap, but her face was rounded and serene, the large brown eyes limpid and full of candour as they gazed up at Robert, who stood in leather jerkin and boots, obviously arrayed for a long journey. Just as she had predicted, he bowed over her hand, holding it a second longer than necessary, pressing the fingers hard. Even as he did so, the sound of light footsteps tripping along the gallery heralded

Elizabeth's approach. She, as always, was finely apparelled, for Elizabeth took unlimited time and care over her toilette. Her hair was unbound and its russet lights were set off by the deep bottle green of her silken gown. Her sleeves were wide and elaborate, lined with primrose figured silk and she wore a ruff, far too elaborate for a morning occasion, but its stiff elaborate height set off the cream complexion, fine features and startling sea-green eyes of the wearer. Elizabeth sparkled with youth and life. 'Robert,' she said. 'Oh, Robert, may I accompany you to Exeter?'

As always, Margaret was offended by her daughter's forward behaviour. Perhaps it was because, in this instance, she was reminded of Nicholas' suggestion that Robert and Elizabeth might marry. She frowned as she recalled her late husband's plans. But she was soon reassured, for Robert said quietly, treating Elizabeth as the child she was, 'Come, chuck, you have to care for your recently widowed mother. Anyway, I am away to London on urgent business. Affairs do not go well there.' And here he turned to Margaret. 'Matters are serious, for the Queen grows old and increasingly besotted with young Essex. Trade flounders, and I must look to our interests.'

Margaret looked up, alert to her business needs. Robert continued, 'I have had words with young Kit and he agrees with me. Indeed he follows close behind and should be with you soon to explain. I hope to look to Nick's affairs, on Kit's behalf.'

'How good you are to us,' said Margaret softly, all jealous thoughts of her daughter dispersed. Indeed the petulant Elizabeth had raced down the stairs and stood in the window embrasure, drumming her fingers on the window. She was thinking, 'How dare he go to London and leave me here! I will show him.' She heard her mother say, 'At least take a draught with us before you go.'

This was Elizabeth's chance; she fled down the passage to the kitchen. She had carried Felicity's potion with her for weeks now. She would put it in his drink and he would return from London and wed her secretly. It was Elizabeth's way always to see things as she wanted them, never as they were. Despite Robert's cool treatment of her since her father's funeral, she could not do other than believe he desired her for his wife. The posset would merely ensure that he would hasten the marriage.

When Elizabeth returned to the Great Hall with a tankard in her hand, a maid following behind with a large pasty and other meats, Kit had arrived. There was little love lost between the two of them, for Kit had long resented Elizabeth's position as her father's favourite. He looked with distaste on his sister's flaunting of her charms. She smiled up at Robert, revealing her sharp white kitten's teeth. She threw back her head to show off the creamy column of her long neck. Robert's eyes dropped to the small childish breasts, peeping from the low-cut gown; hastily he looked away, but Kit had noticed. It was disgusting the way his sister sought to ensnare any man in sight. Even poor steady Tom Gray was not immune. Kit remembered the look of adoration and longing that his friend and companion would throw across the table to where his sister would sit laughing and talking, apparently unconscious of the effect which she was having. Kit knew differently; shut in and reserved himself, he was aware of other people's secret feelings. He knew perfectly well that his sister recognised her own seductive charms. On this occasion he saw Robert turn away, withdraw to that same window embrasure where Elizabeth had recently been sulking. Margaret followed him and they were soon deep in discussion; Kit was summoned across and heard Robert say, 'It is my intention to give up Bourne eventually. I have found a large property in Exeter to replace my present house. I shall make that my home in the West.'

Margaret was silent; she appeared torn and continued to say nothing. So Robert went on, 'Anyway, young Kit here will soon want to set up his own establishment, to marry a rich wife.'

Margaret gazed at her son. It had never even occurred to her that Kit would leave her side. In all the years of Nicholas' wandering and torment, Kit had been there, old beyond his years, to console and counsel his mother. With that same sensitivity which had made him recognise his sister's seductive tactics, Kit now understood his mother's misery and fears. He said reassuringly, 'That is a long time into the future. I have no need to wed.' To himself Kit reflected, 'Nor am I ever likely to.' For he had no interest in women. Beside his mother they seemed to him silly and immature; he always suspected that they were all like Elizabeth beneath the surface. Perhaps it was Kit's solemn looks and stolid reassurance that prompted Margaret to reveal to Kit his inheritance.

That very night, after Robert's departure, in the parlour at High Coombe, set close by the Great Hall, but very private in the fastness of a stout oak door and heavy oak panelling, Margaret ushered her son before the fire, lit to keep out the damp cold of the returning autumn mists. It was very quiet; Elizabeth had long since retired to bed in a sulky humour. As always, Alice and Tim were about their business in kitchen and dairy; in order to rise at dawn, they too would be to their chambers early. The well-trained servants were only to hand if they were summoned. So they were alone.

Margaret looked across the hearth to her handsome son. He held his small head proudly, the shell-like ears close to the tight russet curls. The face was delicate in texture and colour, the mouth like a pink rosebud. For the first time Margaret noted its feminine refinement; she was only too well aware of its sensitivity. She had noted Kit's fastidious withdrawal from the coarse

conversation and even coarser activities of country life,
in complete contrast to Nicholas, who would revel in the
bawdy jokes and lewd gestures of neighbours, as well as
of friends. Margaret could see her son quiver, could
sense the tingling of his skin when he sensed vulgarity,
cruelty or violence. Even now she shivered, wondering
how life would treat one who seemed to lack the
protective covering which kept other people from
undue suffering. For already there was a hint of
melancholy in the boy's whole demeanour, a sense of
withdrawal from his fellow creatures; only with his
wolf-hounds, offspring of Robert's early gift, would Kit
relent and relax, allowing the great creatures to bound
all over him, to lick his face and nestle close to his body.
Sadly, Margaret realised that Kit did not permit even his
mother to fondle or touch him; even now he sat erect
and distant, in the great chair which had once been his
grandfather's. Now she hesitated. "After all," she mused,
"he has a right to know of his truly great heritage."

With this in mind, Margaret began with the Carews
and told him that Nicholas Trenow was the descendant
of that great Cornish family. Kit sat with half-closed
eyes; no hint of any reaction crossed his face. So she
stammered, 'I am telling you this because it does affect
you.'

Here Kit opened his eyes, which were green, blue,
grey opaque, as enigmatic as Kit himself. 'Yes, mother,
yes.'

Margaret drew a deep breath. 'Nicholas Carew
Trenow was your father.'

There was a heavy silence, no sound from without or
within. No breath of wind stirred. The tapestry was still,
even the fire had died to a mass of red ash. The silence
went on. Kit gazed past his mother to the dark
panelling, as if he was tracing every intricate detail of
the carving. A dog stirred at his feet, his wheezy snores
disturbing the silence. Still Kit did not speak. Margaret

clenched her fingers so tight that they were white at the knuckles. Her body was so tense that her shoulders ached. The red ash in the fire collapsed.

Slowly and deliberately, Kit said, 'Why was I never told?'

Margaret released her breath, crossed the room towards Kit. But he turned his whole body away, hid his expression from her and repeated, 'Why was I not told?'

'You were too young.'

'Not too young to run the factors at Topsham, not too young to be at your side when the twins were born, not too young when John drowned and you were inconsolable, not too young when you nearly died after that snowstorm. Never too young for that.' Now his voice rose in an ever louder crescendo.

'That whoreson. That lewd, crude, womanising bastard. That was my father?'

Timidly, Margaret, who had retreated to her chair and sat huddled there said, 'Yes. He was your father. No-one knew. I was married to Richard Bourne six weeks after you were conceived.'

'Thank God for that. I do not want anyone to know that I am of his blood. Understand?'

'Of course, Kit.' Here Margaret began to weep, silent tears to course down her cheeks. Never before had her son been angry with her. She could scarcely remember any anger in him, so closely had Kit commanded his emotions. Now it all spilled over, the resentment, the silent fury of a boy scorned and rejected all his life.

'It was bad enough to be hated when I thought that he was my stepfather. But my own father.' He spat out the words. 'Perhaps he didn't believe you. Perhaps he thought that I was fathered elsewhere.'

The implications of his remark stung Margaret, who turned so white that she seemed likely to swoon at any moment. 'Look at yourself, Kit,' she said. 'You are a Carew through and through. All their aristocratic beauty has flowered in you. Look at your sister. You are like two peas in a pod.'

'I'd rather not,' said Kit grimly. 'I'd rather not.'

'Don't say that, Kit. So much hatred. We are a family, a family.'

Kit ignored her. 'My sister, my sister. He loved her. He hated me. In all the years there was never a kindness, never a word of praise. I tried so often. I worked so hard in the counting house. I took an interest in ships. I mastered the schooling of horses, a task which I found so difficult. But I might as well never have existed.' Now Kit began to sob; dry, harsh sobs without tears. 'I was his own flesh and blood. Yet he never once acknowledged me. Why in God's name did you not tell me?'

Once again, Margaret got up to move closer to him. But now he retreated to the far side of the room, where he stood facing her, his body pressed rigid against the panelling. He too was white, even the skin across the high cheek-bones. You could see what he would look like as an old man, for now he seemed emaciated, as if all the blood had drained away. He seemed to be bone only, no flesh. The eyes were a piercing dark grey, looking through his mother. His hands were stretched out, not in supplication, but to fend her off, to reject her advances.

Margaret dropped at his feet. 'I thought that you would despise me, for letting your father have his way. I was a great lady, not some servant girl to give in to passion.'

Coldly, Kit said, 'You are a great lady, strong, intelligent, beautiful, far too good for the likes of him.' He paused. 'We will never discuss it again. Do you understand?' He turned, blundering in the shadows towards the door. Margaret remained crumpled on the floor. The tears were dry, even weeping was no longer possible. It seemed as though all her past life lay in ruins, all wasted.

Hearing the young master ride away into the night, the servants came and found Margaret. Devoted as always, they carried her to her bed, to the same bedchamber where all her children, save one, had been conceived.

It was a measure of Margaret's strength that she rose early next morning and set about her household duties. Her pallor was noted by her servants and by the devoted Alice and Tim. Elizabeth failed to notice, for she rode out with her favourite hawk. Kit did not return for three days and when he did he silenced his mother with a look. He bowed and said, 'We must to London, my dear, for Robert was right. We are needed there far more than here, where affairs seem settled. Alice and Tim can cope with the estate. All the factors at Topsham and Exeter have their orders.'

Margaret noted the stern visage, the upright carriage. Her heart ached for her son, to see him aged ten years in a week. It was true that when they arrived in London, fellow merchants, servants, factors, all believed that they had been mistaken and that Master Christopher Bourne was a man in his late twenties. Neither Kit nor Margaret disillusioned them.

13   New Lives

In late November Robert returned to Bourne, intent upon consolidating his business in Exeter. Meanwhile he was ready to reorganise the household in his old home and to set in hand a vast movement of goods and chattels in the early spring. As he rode down the valley, he was humming to himself. Despite the damp and inauspicious weather, he felt exhilarated. Always optimistic and cheerful, his spirits were higher than ever. It is natural when an old friend dies to mourn, but also natural to rejoice in one's own survival. The future looked rosy. Despite the threat of the old Queen's passing, so devastated was she at the death of Leicester, Parliament looked ready to cope with any situation. Robert was full of energy, brimming over with vitality.

This is how Elizabeth found him when she braved the first snow to ride over to Bourne, hearing the servants talk of his return and his preparations for a move into Exeter. The prospect pleased her. Although she enjoyed hawking and hunting, as well as all the equestrian pursuits of High Coombe's great stud, she loved the company and the entertainments of a great town house. She saw herself as Robert's wife, entertaining his friends in London as well as Exeter; he would take her to Court as well where she would be the centre of admiring young men. Once Robert had his heir, he would allow his wife anything, jewels, fortune, clothes and, above all, the freedom of a changing and enjoyable life, such as she had glimpsed at Lady Letitia's

So Elizabeth day-dreamed, as she hastened towards her lover, through the woods. Heavy with child, she rode cautiously over the frozen ground and the treacherous patches of ice, which were the offspring of nearby streams. Skeletal black branches hung low and were glittering with frost. Wintry sunlight had melted this in patches and droplets of water clutched at her face and hood. She was oblivious to discomfort, although her feet were frozen and her hands numb, so numb inside her gloves that she was hard put to keep a grip on the reins. But she had chosen a sure-footed and sturdy mare from their extensive stables and the horse picked her way down the last slope into the courtyard at Bourne.

Dismounting carefully, Elizabeth wrapped her cloak tightly around her. She would hide her condition, although all at High Coombe knew about her pregnancy, almost from the moment of her mother's departure for London. Elizabeth thought angrily, 'She never noticed me anyway. I only had to keep to my wing of the house. She and Kit seemed absorbed in their own thoughts. She scarcely enquired after me.' So it was that she was thinking of her mother when she entered Bourne, through a side door.

Robert was at home. Elizabeth could hear his deep voice booming orders to his great mastiffs, and, as she threw open the door, she became aware of a gust of warm air from the brilliant fire, which illuminated the whole dark room. Robert himself was ablaze too in an enormous doublet of purple, slashed with silver. His hose was cross-gartered in silver and gold. From his neck hung a jewelled pomander and it sparkled in the firelight. From his bearded face shone out the dark eyes, full of life and laughter.

Robert advanced to meet her and said in a hearty

voice, 'Elizabeth, my dear. This is a dreadful day to ride over, so overcast too.'

'Talk not of the weather, my darling.' And Elizabeth, still dripping wet, threw herself into his arms. So sudden was the movement that he stumbled backwards, unconsciously noting the weight of her.

He righted his balance and took her by the shoulders. 'Steady, my chuck. Steady. Come and dry by the fire.'

'Oh Robert. Do not be so composed. Are you not pleased to see me? I love you, my sweeting. I love you.'

Her lover turned away, almost embarrassed. 'My dear Elizabeth, calm yourself.'

Then her control gave way. All the worry of the last months in his absence from her, her concern that she should have declared herself before his departure for London, came out in a torrent of words. In truth she had dreaded her mother's tongue and her brother's scorn; she had planned to meet Robert alone, a secret marriage so that no-one need ever know that her child had been conceived outside wedlock. But she had fretted for Robert's return. Now his cool reception upset her youthful and decidedly unbalanced emotions. 'Marry me, Robert. Marry me.'

Robert paled. 'I am too old, older than your father. We must find a young sprig.'

Elizabeth sobbed. 'You are not too old. You are so virile, so handsome. You must marry me.' Here she threw back her cloak, revealing her swollen belly.

Robert eyed her condition with horror, a fact that did not escape her notice. Her voice became hysterical. 'Robert, what is it? Don't you love me?'

Her lover swept her into his arms, kissing her eyes and mouth. Always kindly, Robert was shamed to his very soul. Who would have thought this child could be pregnant as a result of a moment's madness?

He whispered softly into her ear. She shrieked and the servants came running. Abruptly, he gestured them away and ordered the dogs down, as they too rose in alarm at the hysterical girl.

Now Robert sat by the fire, throwing off her cloak, cradling her and crooning to her, stroking her forehead and her lovely tumbled hair. 'Elizabeth, my love, I am married. I am so sorry.'

Now she turned her face up to him, her voice no longer muffled in the fastness of his chest. 'Married already? How can you be? The Lady Eleanor is dead.'

'Not the Lady Eleanor. I married your mother three weeks ago.'

At the back of her mind she was saying to herself, 'The love philtre. That is why he married my mother.' Then in the agony of the moment, the thought was lost.

Robert felt her body stiffen and saw her eyes glare. 'That plain dumpy old woman. You preferred her to me.' She began to scream again, to hurl abuse, language which he heard only in the stables, or the stews of Exeter and London. He saw her face hard and vicious, the mouth drawn down, the eyes spiteful. In the midst of his confusion and apprehension he could yet hear an inner voice whispering, 'This one is a real shrew. What have I escaped?'

Years ago in this very room his own impetuous behaviour had made him drive out wife and children, four fine sons, all lost for ever, three of the fever and one to the Pope. He would not repeat his mistake. He continued to rock Elizabeth, to wipe her face, to croon endearments.

Meanwhile he was thinking hard. Margaret must never know. Nor must the world. Thank God he had sent away the servants. Out loud, he said cautiously, 'We must find you a husband.'

It was unfortunate that Elizabeth looked up to see the expression on his face. She was of tender years, she had only seen the bluff, good-looking, humorous side of Robert Fursdon. Now she caught the measure of a shrewd, calculating self-interest. She shivered and detached herself from his grasp. She said stiffly and with pride, 'There is one who will marry me, who will do anything for me.'

'And who is that, sweetheart?'

'Tom Gray.'

Robert felt a pang that this daughter of a great house should be sacrificed to a menial. It was but momentary; he was still in a panic about Margaret. He must get the girl away before her mother could meet up with her.

This time when Robert rode to High Coombe, it was with quiet deliberation. the household was asleep, the servants knew him and directed him to Tom's lonely chamber. Robert's only words were, 'Elizabeth has sent me. She needs you.' The young man said nothing, but dressing quickly, mounted his horse and set off for Bourne.

Tom was well aware of Elizabeth's condition, but he was deeply in love with her. He had adored her ever since his arrival at High Coombe. He guessed at the paternity of the child and had believed that Robert would make her his wife. As they rode, Robert explained the whole situation. Now Tom learnt that his beloved foster-mother was at risk, as Robert's new bride, and he agreed to give out that he and Elizabeth had been secretly married in the spring. Meanwhile he took his childhood sweetheart away to The Netherlands, exulting in the fact that she was his at last, confident that her gratitude would turn to love.

* * *

Robert's own feelings were mixed as he stood on the quay at Topsham and watched their ship gain speed as the wind filled out the sails. It was a fine fast craft and was soon out of sight. Robert's first reaction was one of overwhelming relief; he had given Tom sufficient money to keep the young couple away for a considerable time. Now he was free to conclude his business in Exeter and to return to his wife as quickly as possible. 'His wife. His beloved Margaret.' Here was confusion. He loved the gracious tranquil lady and had done so for years; her quiet nature matched exactly the volatile tempestuous quality of his own personality. She soothed him whenever his temper threatened to flair; she calmed him at times of crisis, when responsibilities seemed daunting. She listened and advised but never ordered. She would divert conflict with a quiet joke; she would direct his servants, as she did her own, so that they adored her. This was no mean achievement in a household which had lacked a mistress for years. His marriage therefore was no mistake. Why then did he feel an aching regret? That chit Elizabeth would have proved a most unsatisfactory partner in every respect. She was haughty and tactless, domineering, demanding satisfaction of every passing whim and fancy. She had no interest in his business and no capacity for diplomacy. But my God she was beautiful!

On board ship returning to London, Robert had plenty of time to dwell on her remarkable complexion and colouring, her small childish breasts, her long slender figure. He could see those enchanting eyes, one moment green and the next blue or grey. The winged eyebrows were equally mobile and revealed her changing moods. Then too he would recall her pregnancy; this was his greatest regret, for his desire for a male heir was overwhelming. He had been quite calculating in assessing Margaret's capacity for childbearing, had noted that she always quickened on Nicholas' infrequent visits, that her children were usually vigorous and healthy; her standing in the West Country and her fortune were undeniable assets. But now the fact remained that Elizabeth was pregnant and his wife was not.

Margaret in her great London home was blissfully

unaware of Robert's turmoil. So desperately was she in love with her husband that she had scarcely eaten or slept since his sudden departure. His decision to pay a lightning visit to Bourne and Exeter so soon after their wedding had proved a bitter blow, for he had seemed as content as she. So swift had been their courtship and so rushed the ceremony that she had recognised in him an impatience as great as her own. And it had led her into further dispute with her beloved Kit.

For Kit had been both amazed and horrified when Margaret had announced her plans. His resentment had been the greater because he recognised events as being very much the result of his own actions. He had sought to dispel the misery brought on by Margaret's revelation of his paternity by throwing himself feverishly into the reorganisation of Nicholas' London business. He had laboured from dawn to dusk. He had become aware that his father (wryly he used that term) had dabbled in business of all kinds, grocery and haberdashery – imports of pins, needles, knives, leather buckets as well as spices, oils and currants. Nicholas had little interest in wool or cloth, and had not built up a trade in undyed cloth, such as Robert Fursdon. Robert was a prominent member of the Merchant Adventurers, and engaged in the import of silks of all kinds, damask, satin and velvet. Kit had noticed how finely his mother was dressed from the moment of their arrival at his lodgings in Cheapside. He gave little thought to the bearer of these gifts. But he had determined to link their woollen trade in the West to a brisk commerce in London. He was even anxious to get involved in the Royal Exchange and so learn more of finance. He wanted to extend the shipbuilding interests on the Thames and link them with the Topsham activities. It had not seemed to matter that the London fortune was Margaret's and the Topsham his own. They seemed identical until Margaret announced her intention of marrying Robert.

Kit had always loved the big giant, who had taken more notice of him than Nicholas Trenow himself. Initially it was because Robert was at High Coombe more than its master. Kit was ever one to be at his mother's side when enterprises such as weaving were discussed; he was inducted into the mysteries of hawking and hunting by Margaret, who shared much of that with her neighbours, especially Robert Fursdon. Robert who had made Kit a present of his first hawk and later of that wolf-hound puppy, who was the patriarch of a fine pack. Francis Fursdon had been Kit's boon companion but Kit's resentment of Robert's anti-papist stand was long since gone. He came to understand the Catholic menace and, a fine scholar himself, could see the divergence between the Catholic creed and the more prosaic and pragmatic Anglican approach to religion. More significantly, Kit was sensitive to the feelings which bound Francis to his mother and alienated him from his father. So Kit did not object to Robert as a man; he appreciated his kindness and his generosity. But he was a youth reared to refined manners and to a strict etiquette. His mother was barely two months a widow, and she proposed to marry a close friend of her husband's.

Margaret loved her son as she loved no other person. She felt for him in all his trials, but she did not share his concern for other people's opinions. This was because she was a Penhale and, in the West Country, whatever they did was right and acceptable. After all, her marriage to Nicholas had followed in indecent haste after Richard Bourne's death. She had weathered the criticism and found that neighbours and friends soon forgot the scandal. She could scarcely remind her son of that event, so fraught with implications for himself. But she could point out to Kit that Margaret Penhale Trenow was unknown in London and Robert so prominent that his popularity and wealth would be a protection for her reputation. She laughed gently and said, 'Kit, we are no spring chickens, you know.' Her son did not even smile; he replied stiffly, 'I cannot give you my approval or my blessing. I shall return to the West Country and leave your London affairs in the capable hands of your new husband.'

At Margaret's request, Robert too was very gentle with his new stepson. He begged him to stay, announcing that he had no intention of taking over the management of Margaret's affairs, if Kit would continue. Indeed Kit had largely followed Robert's advice in plans to expand and link activities and trade in London and Topsham. But Kit could not be persuaded and he had left almost immediately after the wedding, but he had not been in Topsham to attend his sister's secret wedding, as he had departed for France some weeks before; France, where political affairs were in turmoil and where Kit and other Exeter merchants had to reorganise the considerable wine trade which plied between north-western France and Exeter.

It was the greater shock to Margaret that Robert should choose to leave her alone, when Kit had already deserted her. But it had been Robert's turn to laugh. 'Alone? My dear Margaret, this great house is full of servants, all of whom already adore you and are waiting for you to give your orders and turn this place into another High Coombe.'

Margaret's face turned pale. High Coombe. That it would never be.

Robert was too impatient to notice his wife's reaction. At no time did he appreciate her love for her estates, which was almost an obsession. He had not been born and bred to the land as she had been, nor did he share her love of the countryside and all its inhabitants. So he refused to allow her to accompany him to Devon in mid-winter. The journey was too hazardous. He could travel on any ship, with little or no degree of comfort;

he would not subject his wife, reared in luxury, to such a trial. He promised to return quickly to her side, explaining how impatient he was to sort out the new mansion in Exeter.

It was Margaret's turn to reflect, upon her love for this new husband. So skilled was his lovemaking, so tender and yet so demanding, that she wondered at the years of Nicholas' casual and intermittent courting. For apart from the journey west, Robert seemed entirely preoccupied in making her happy. They would lie abed like any couple in the first flush of youth; he would caress and whisper endearments. He would praise her beauty and describe in minute detail all her qualities of honesty, tenderness and kindness. He would constantly praise her quiet soul. He lavished presents upon her – jewels and gowns such as she had never owned. The Devon jenny-wren should become the London swan. Indeed she would watch those lovely creatures on the river which swirled past the end of their beautiful garden. She would vow never to eat their flesh. Robert would laugh and sit her in the love-seat, which was positioned behind the yew hedge. He would nibble at her ear and tease, saying that her flesh was just as tender and must be tasted. She would run her fingers through his beard, saying that he was as tough as any wild boar and just as dangerous, whereupon he would carry her to bed, pretending to ravish her. For the first time in her life she felt beloved and special; when he left, she found the parting intolerable and kept to her bedchamber. Then she remembered his desire for a perfectly run household. Once again the jenny-wren returned, so she clothed herself in fustian, put on a plain cap and, despite the winter weather, turned out the whole house. Never had there been such a shining and a polishing, never had rushes been changed so frequently, tapestries were taken down and relocated. She even had craftsmen in to regild the chambers. Little food could be purchased in mid-winter, but the cooks could be instructed in new spicy dishes; pastries and possets of the West Country cider, brought up to Cheapside, were transported to Robert's home and used to enliven salted and spiced meats. When Robert returned he was delighted and turned his attention to entertainment, for the wedding had been quick and three weeks of undivided attention for his bride had excluded neighbours and colleagues. Now Robert would show off his wife and his new household. His colleagues in the Merchant Adventurers, wealthy as they were, were astounded at the display and the entertainment.

14   London

The new gold leaf was a tremendous success. The Great
Hall had a magnificent plastered ceiling, now adorned
in a Renaissance style with azure and scarlet. As a
surprise, Margaret had inserted the coats of arms of
Carews, Bohuns, Penhales and the new blazon of the
Fursdons, which was of three fleeces and a ram's horn,
scarlet on purple. The lozenge over the fine central
fireplace was quartered with an enormous heraldic
display. Nothing that she could have done would have
pleased him more. Both husband and wife knew that
the marriage had cemented two great fortunes and that
the Penhale-Fursdon alliance was now a power in the
land.

To herald Robert's return, Margaret planned an
enormous banquet, to which all his acquaintances were
summoned, and the core of those invited were the
Merchant Adventurers, those wealthy and successful
traders in the country's finest product, wool. But the
gathering also included all members of the Common
Council and the powerful leaders of other guilds.
Haberdashers', Apothecaries', Fishmongers', Tanners',
Silversmiths', Goldsmiths' and many others. None could
or would refuse such an invitation. The women wore
the highest and stiffest ruffs or collars, the most brilliant
peacock hues of silks and satins, immense farthingales
over embroidered petticoats. Both men and women
displayed vast jewelled sleeves, so large and so heavy,

that plenty of space had to be set aside at the tables, groaning under the dishes which were carried on high by processions of servants, liveried in purple and scarlet, Robert's colours. There were oysters, salmon, whiting, turkeys, hens, capons, pigeons, a haunch of beef, and mutton, mallards, teals, snytes. The greatest delicacy were herons. But there were prunes, raisins, marchpanes and rich cream in abundance. Being mid-winter most dishes were spiced, including sampere, a maritime rock plant, the leaves of which were pickled in vinegar.

The farthingales tended not to be the new Spanish variety but the old 'bum-roll' type and the men wore the huge padded doublets rather than the new canions, but these guests were of that generation of the high Elizabethan age. So entertainment too was of the ancient kind, tumblers, jesters and troupes of dancers. It was Margaret's genius to have provided Morris dancers, imported from the country, who proved a great success. The light steps of their nimble feet, the great clanging of wooden staves, the colourful interplay of swirling ribbons, recalled for many a man and woman the days of their youth, for a number of these merchants were self-made men, like Robert, who had come from up-country to seek their fortune in the capital. They had worked hard to achieve fame and fortune and now they were set to enjoy it. Ales, wines and cider, imported from High Coombe, flowed freely; the jokes became bawdier and the voices louder.

Robert's face was flushed and his booming voice as resonant as any present. Forgotten was Elizabeth and her toils, forgotten the unborn child stirring in her womb; looking at his dignified wife, clad so richly in her favourite apricot velvet and emerald bedecked stomacher, Robert's heart leapt for joy. 'Come, chuck,' he said. 'Send for the musicians. You and I shall dance a galliard in celebration of this day.' The castellated arms of the Penhales winked down at the handsome couple, he of such a size that they stood out from their guests, for Robert was clad entirely in white and many commented on his likeness to the great Robert Dudley. Margaret's steps were not quite as high as those of the great Elizabeth, but many there recognised in her a veritable queen of the revels.

The last guest did not depart until the early hours and Margaret must supervise the clearing of the floor. Indeed a few men, so far gone in their cups that they had dropped where they stood, were carried to distant chambers. The dogs had eaten their fill of discarded meats. The swimming fantasies of dissolving confections were hurriedly disposed of; the crowning glory of a dish artfully fashioned in the form of a flock of sheep, so designed as a compliment to the Merchant Adventurers, was given to the kitchen lads and apprentices who had laboured over the kitchen fires all night. Margaret had a word even for the least of them, and, as she finally climbed the stairs to the bedchamber, a fitful January sun streamed through the fine window and illuminated the great stone staircase, which ran across the back of the hall. Here the roof was timbered in the finest English oak, but still adorned with carved heraldic devices. How proud Robert was to display the ancient Bohun arms. Margaret smiled to herself, for she understood the dreams of the Cornish fisherman's son. As she entered their chamber, she could hear his snores and saw that he lay back, arms outstretched in all his sartorial splendour. She closed the bed-curtains again and crossed to the small pallet bed in a retiring room close by. She was awakened by his roars, 'Meg. Meg, for God's sake, woman. Where are you? I want you here,' and he blundered into the dark recess where she lay; throwing back the fur coverlet, he knelt to caress her plump limbs and pink-nippled breasts. He cursed as he strove to undo his points. She laughed as she moved languorously across the room to climb up into the enormous four-poster bed. Now he was naked and, hearing her soft laughter, said in a menacing tone, 'How dare you thwart me in my desires, you witch?' Whereupon she drew up her arms and clasped him tightly around the neck. She was still full of sleep and so it seem that their coming together was like a dream. He seemed to move in slow motion, as he gently disentangled those imprisoning hands. He reared his head and lowered himself into her. It was measured, and she felt wave upon wave of desire. 'Wait,' she cried, until thunderously and inevitably they met in the full glory of a final ecstasy, simultaneously achieved for both of them. They slept in each other's arms, until late in the dark winter afternoon Robert, clad in a scarlet bedgown, brought her ale and titbits of chicken, salted fish and marchpane. There were no candles, only an enormous fire in the great chimney. Bed-curtains were drawn back and she lounged against the bolster, licking her lips. In the dusk and the flickering firelight, she was a young girl again, or so it seemed to her infatuated lover. Her pink tongue was like a kitten's, savouring every morsel. She smiled and lowered her lids; she knew what was to come, and so it was, for they made love all night. She wondered at his energy, as he rose to go to the counting house next morning, whilst she lay abed and slept. The servants smiled knowingly; the great household went about its tasks, pleased that the master was back and the mistress content.

Margaret needed that sleep, for the lovemaking continued and was interspersed with bouts of hospitality from Robert's friends, who sought unsuccessfully to outdo him in the provision of banquets and entertainments. The women looked enviously at Margaret, noting the secret looks between husband and wife. They had no eyes for anyone else. Nubile daughters brought forth to be displayed in a marriage market pouted at

Robert's lack of interest, for, before Margaret's advent, the ever popular giant was wont to chuck them under the chin or pinch their bottoms, flirting outrageously with all the pretty girls. Merchants' wives commented maliciously upon Margaret's advancing years and large fortune. 'I can understand why he married her. But why is he so besotted? She looks plain enough to me, a quiet country housewife.' Or another would say, 'He needs an heir badly. I wonder that he did not look for someone younger.' Then they would glance at their elderly husbands, with their protruding stomachs and balding heads, and sigh in envy.

Margaret remained unconscious of the gossip. She was blissfully happy. And this despite her surroundings, for cocooned in the grandeur and ostentation of the great house Margaret still could not like the City. A cleanly soul, reared at High Coombe, surrounded by hills, woods and fields, she and Robert could only ride out through filthy, odorous streets, thronged with vociferous apprentices, bustling market women and, above all, beggars. They came in all shapes and sizes, tiny children exploited by their parents with suppurating sores, wizened creatures foaming at the mouth, either simulating fits or actually having them, dark satanic villains who ran at her stirrup demanding alms. She fed as many as thronged at her kitchen door, as she did at High Coombe, but they were so numerous, so all-persuasive in the streets, that she was sickened to the stomach. In Exeter, where indeed there was poverty, North Street or Eastgate seemed full of prosperous citizens going about their business, but wherever she went in London, the criminals and the poor pursued her, or so it seemed to the gentle and kindly Margaret. The stocks were always full. The gibbets bent under their grisly burdens. London Bridge was adorned with dried and wizened heads of traitors. Robert would warn her of the cozening that went on, of those who would steal washing off the line or pretend to be legless or armless sailors, back from the wars; but she could never close her heart to their appeals and he loved her for it.

So when Robert took her at Easter down the Strand to the Chamber of Common Council to meet his fellow aldermen and the Mayor and to watch the guild's mystery plays, he was well aware that she was haunted by the suffering, however spurious, of those around her. She enjoyed the spectacle of the gentle Virgin, clad in blue, and happy tears came to her eyes at the sight of the babe. She rejoiced to see Christ turn the money-sellers from the temple. She could even laugh at the antics of those in the wicker basket, representing Hell, those who peeped out in supplication to be released from their torments. But she wept and would not look at the agony of Gethsemane. She moved away when a procession was formed and the young man, portraying Christ, had ox-blood on his forehead and laboured to carry the Cross the length of the Strand. Robert sought her out, smiling, 'Come love. Our Lord is restored in all His glory.' And so he was, with gentle angels to either hand, as he was lifted on a creaking device to represent Ascension. Neighbours smiled at Margaret's tears, but, despite their envy, liked this quiet woman, who was ever ready to help with a herbal remedy if a child was ill or to hasten over with some gift if there was a family celebration. The Penhale heiress was never proud or arrogant, never boasted of wealth or fortune, only of her husband's virtues. This was met with knowing smiles. They knew a likeable rogue when they met one. But let the lady nurse her idyll, whilst she could. But then came the realisation of her husband's dreams, for they were summoned to Court.

At the mystery plays, Margaret had enjoyed the antics of the artisans. They put her in mind of Bottom the Weaver and his friends, for Robert had taken her to the Globe. He had also escorted her to the home of the Earl of Southampton and a performance of *Richard II*. Robert told her that his invitation had come because of the Bohun connection and it led to Robert's introduction to Court. Where Robert Fursdon on his own was scorned as a 'parvenue', his marriage to a Penhale heiress and his new link with the Carews had made nobles like Southampton review their prejudice. After all, the fellow was useful for a loan or two, for Robert, like many another merchant, dabbled in usury. The Queen's demands, her fabulous progresses, kept her courtiers poor and they had need of alternate sources of revenue, like trade. Indeed Margaret had made Robert wince when she said quietly one day, 'Elizabeth could well have married into the nobility had she wanted.' Robert could not bear to reply; anyway it was only a few days afterwards that the summons to Greenwich came.

The sickening and ageing Queen was loath to create more knights, but a substantial sum from the Fursdon purse, which could be put to use in the Irish wars, together with the Earl of Southampton's patronage, eased Robert's way and he could at last kneel at Margaret's feet, a twinkle in his eye, and call her, 'My Lady'. What is more, the very next day he carried her in their new boat up river to Greenwich. It was a fine barge, decorated with lambs' heads and gilded with trellises of carved ivy and forget-me-nots. It was propelled smoothly by a sturdy crew of purple-liveried boatmen, who took her skilfully beneath the arches of London Bridge. Margaret could not help but wonder at Robert's boldness in so attiring his servants, for she remembered her father's cautionary tales of Tudor laws against livery and maintenance. She reminded herself that nothing could now threaten that lady, so deeply enthroned in the hearts of her people. The old nobility were gone, beheaded or impoverished beyond recall. Now men like Robert were Elizabeth's henchmen, devoted to her Protestant cause against the ever present danger of French or Spanish domination.

Nervously, Margaret lifted her heavy skirts as she mounted the slippery steps at the side of Greenwich Palace. She was clad in her favourite velvet, this time of a soft moss green. At Robert's request she was dressed simply with few jewels, for the Queen disliked any woman, particularly if they were young, to compete with her. But Robert, in his Queen's honour, could go displayed in the richest damask and silver cloth. His breeches were adorned with silver canions. He wore a large feathered cap, which he used in a magnificent gesture of bowing before his sovereign. The feathers from a peacock's tail, all colours of the rainbow, would catch the ultramarine of his fine hose with jewelled garters of opal and turquoise.

Margaret gasped to see the blaze of jewels which was the Queen. She almost had to shade her eyes, so dazzling was the display. The royal dress was encrusted with pearls and diamonds, the thin elegant white hands covered with rings. Then Margaret looked into the enamelled face and saw the tired eyes. They reminded her of that long-lost spaniel, 'Jess', who, when she had been sick of some bilious complaint, had looked wont to die. Then the Queen turned, in a lazy gesture, to the most beautiful young man at her side, Robert Devereux, and he said something softly which made her smile. The monarch's glance slid over Margaret and came to rest on Robert's glorious figure. Margaret could sense the Queen saying to herself, 'Here is a man.' It was true that the over-elaborate costume set off the broad shoulders, powerful chest and sturdy legs to perfection. 'The Queen did ever favour virility,' Margaret thought. Then the monarch was gone out of sight, into an inner chamber. It seemed as though the light went with her, although a thousand wax candles blazed, for Elizabeth I hated and feared darkness. The musicians played gavottes and galliards, but there was no dancing, for the

Queen could no longer display her talents in that direction. They waited and Margaret's legs began to ache and she felt a little faint; she glanced at Robert, but he stood triumphantly arrogant in the midst of that brilliant throng.

In the future, whenever Margaret heard a particular plaintive tune on the dulcimer, she would recall the sadness of that moment, for she had no doubt that they were all witnessing the passing of an era; but she held her peace, recognising that for Robert it was the culmination of a lifetime's ambition. Secretly she hugged to herself the thought that she had it in her power to crown it all.

15 *The Heir*

Margaret was very weary when they finally returned home from the Court, but Robert obviously felt so excited that he must talk about his experiences. 'Oh, my darling, you don't know how long I have waited for this. When I married Eleanor, I expected it all to happen, but Eleanor's guardians were anxious to send us off to the country and to forget about the fisherman's son to whom they had espoused their royal ward.' Robert could not prevent bitterness creeping into his tone. This surprised Margaret, who had not heard her husband speak of the past at all. She had no idea that he nursed such resentment, although she was well aware of his overwhelming ambition. It saddened her to hear him talk of Lady Eleanor in that context, for the lady had been a good friend and Margaret had nursed guilty thoughts about her subsequent relationship with Eleanor's husband. It was ridiculous, for she and Robert had only become really close companions after his wife's departure. Yet Margaret had hid from herself the real concern which she had felt for Eleanor's incarceration. It was hard to reconcile this with Robert's essentially kindly nature, but she had striven to understand his deep sense of betrayal. Most of all, Margaret recognised the threat which Eleanor's Catholicism posed to Robert's standing and fortune, which he had laboured to build up over many years. If Robert had mistreated his first wife he had paid deeply in the alienation of his

168

sons. Margaret was roused from this reverie by the sight of Robert pacing the bedchamber, as the first hint of light crept through the enormous bay window. In the greyness of dawn he had a shadowy image and Margaret shivered. 'Come to bed, my love. All is well for you. The Queen noted your person and in the City all know what that knighthood betokens. In the west, your heirs will carry a great name.'

Robert turned and peered at her. To her amazement, his first query was, 'Madam, do you refer to the proud Penhales or to my own race?'

Margaret had thought that he might guess the significance of her words and, in her fatigue, her stomach turned queasy at his jealous tone. This was a side of Robert she had never seen. She climbed out of bed and crossed the room to lay her fingers on his lips. 'The Penhale Fursdons, my darling. And if you are not to bed, the first of them may grow so weary that he may decide he is not for this world.' She saw his face lighten and a great beaming smile creased the beloved features. He lifted her off her feet and leapt around the room in a great galliard. 'Meg, you have done it. You have done it.'

Laughing, she said, 'Put me down, sirrah. I believe you had a hand in it too.'

Margaret was disappointed that he did not make love to her. But that was to be the pattern of the months ahead. He treated her as if she was a piece of Venetian glass or more likely a precious egg, so fragile that she must nestle in some feathered nest, until she was ready to bring forth that which he desired above all things. They were too old to be so foolish and yet they talked of the babe as the heir; neither admitted that it could be a girl. After all, Robert had only fathered sons on the Lady Eleanor and Margaret had but one daughter. Robert would come into his wife's bedchamber every morning and give instructions for her care, then he would leave to meet up with other merchants or to supervise his cargoes; it was obvious that he had neglected his affairs in these last six months.

Margaret became unhappy, for the jenny-wren felt caged. She might not venture abroad, for Robert would not have her astride a horse. The carriage was as confined as the house. Summer came on and it grew very hot; even in the garden the air was heavy and stifling; no breath of wind stirred the still murky waters of the river. Margaret would wander, disconsolate, aware that her burgeoning figure was matched in a swelling of the face. Margaret had ever seen herself as plain and unattractive, until Robert had made her feel differently. Now Robert could no longer liken her to a swan. She walked clumsily and had to pause for breath after a few steps; so large was she that she began to wonder if it was twins again. Robert was kindness itself, but he was seldom there. She felt ugly and rejected; she longed for home. Sitting behind the yew hedge where she and Robert had shared their joke about the swan, she began to dream of High Coombe. She tasted the breath of the sweet clear west wind, she smelt the bracken and that deep intangible tang of red Devon soil. She smelt the new-mown hay and heard the night owls and the swish of wings as the herons swept over the River Exe.

'My love, you are dreaming. It is growing dark.' Robert was there, kneeling at her feet and, as she opened her eyes, he was horrified to see tears coursing down her cheeks.

'I dreamt that I was home.'

Robert had been sure that Margaret was pining for High Coombe and the health of the babe was ever his first concern. He could see that Margaret drooped in the heat. Only today he had heard of a few cases of the plague in the crowded streets behind the Shambles. That had decided him. Gently, he said, 'Darling, I have a ship sailing for Topsham next week. The weather is so good and the sea so calm that you may go aboard and be at High Coombe within the month.'

Margaret smiled through her tears. 'Robert, you are so good to me. I shall miss you, my dear. Oh, how I shall miss you. No-one could have given me more love or care, and I do mean in the months before this young man showed himself.' Here she patted her belly. 'Your concern for me was always there, even before I did as I was commanded and quickened.' She smiled gently.

That night, supper was served in her chamber. Robert sat and amused her with stories of their neighbours. 'Old Giles Trenway has never been on board in his life. He decides to inspect the cargo, trips over a rope and lies spread-eagled on deck. He is so fat that he cannot heave his great paunch up, and the sailors try to hide their laughs when they see him floundering in wet tar. He compounds the joke by swearing vigorously.'

'Poor Giles,' said Margaret. 'He is so proud.'

'But pride comes before a fall.'

Dusk crept on and a hauntingly beautiful summer night hid the stench and ugliness of the City. The river was silver in the moonlight. Margaret cupped Robert's face in her hands. 'My love. Oh, my love.'

Robert stroked her cheeks and touched her breasts. He held her gently till she slept and crept back to his own bed in the front of the house.

It was a memory that Margaret treasured in the months ahead. High Coombe was as she imagined it. All the servants crowded to the terrace on her arrival, including the hounds and even her own mare, thoughtfully led to the front of the house by her old friend Luke. He tried to hide his concern to see his mistress so swollen and dropsical. But the clear clean sea breezes did wonders for her. She could sleep with windows open and hear the nightingales. Even the owls were her friends and their raucous calls were welcome to her ears.

Margaret missed Robert dreadfully but Kit was a regular visitor; all the old disputes were forgotten. He was as solicitous as Robert, giving careful instructions to Alice about the food, which must be prepared to tempt her appetite, for even in later pregnancy she felt nauseous. The swelling in her ankles continued to be troublesome. Kit tried to keep neighbours and friends at arm's length but it was difficult because Margaret had always been very popular and acquaintances were interested in this union of two well-known figures in the locality. Robert's ears must have burned, for Margaret's devotion was a favourite topic in Devon cottages and mansion. 'Poor love, she deserves well,' said the blacksmith's wife. 'He was a real rogue, old Nicholas Trenow.' Lady Pentle at Westham Castle commented sourly, 'Not much to choose between them – Nicholas Trenow and Sir Robert Fursdon. Sir Robert indeed and he a fisherman's son.' Margaret was having the Fursdon coat of arms blazoned on chimney breasts and ceilings at High Coombe. In Exeter, Robert's grand mansion, close to the newly opened water-gate, was taking shape and seemed likely to prove one of the largest in the town. Fellow City Councillors commented on its proximity to the quay and understood that Robert, like themselves, wanted to see his ships sail all the way up to Exeter, as they used to do a hundred years before. But people wondered at his continuing absence, as the birth date drew near.

Margaret moved even more slowly but showed herself at harvest supper and was enthusiastic about winter sowing. It had been a great harvest, barns were overflowing and young Tim and Alice worked with a will in dairy and slaughter-house, in still room and mill. Margaret was touched by their devotion. She was not too sick herself to give attention to the stud and to make new plans for breeding. She enjoyed supervising the cider-making, and the smells of crushed apple seemed to ease her biliousness. She missed Tom Gray, but in her heart of hearts she was glad to be rid of the tempestuous Elizabeth. When Robert had finally braced himself to tell her of the runaway marriage and, in a subsequent confession, of a goodly sum to be expended on a journey overseas, Margaret could not bring herself to criticise her husband or her nephew, for she loved Tom and could see that he would be close-bound by further family ties to High Coombe and its affairs, once he returned. He was stolid and strong, could be relied on to support her daughter in all her moods. Elizabeth's dowry, as yet untouched, would provide for her daughter's extravagant way of life. She began to plan to make over a whole wing at High Coombe for their use.

Kit was remarkably close on the subject, replying in monosyllables to all Margaret's questions and queries about the future of Elizabeth and Tom Gray. Kit had his own suspicions but he kept them to himself, and thanked God that everyone else accepted the story that Tom was Elizabeth's lover. Margaret was used to the taciturn Kit and put the continuing silence down to jealousy of his sister.

It was unfortunate that Kit had to return on urgent business to France, where the turn of political events kept the wine trade in a turmoil. The assassination of the French king had brought further violence and bloodshed: Margaret was aware of events and worried about Kit's safety. 'Mother, no-one cares a hoot about an obscure Englishman, who keeps himself to himself. Anyway the Frenchman always wants to turn a sou into a franc, and I shall be there to relieve them of their precious wine.' Margaret had to be content but, in the same month after his departure, went into a very prolonged labour. Her child was eventually born in late November.

Robert had not been indifferent to his wife: indeed he was also anxious to see how the building at Exeter was going, so he tried to get away to the west. Events conspired against him; war with Spain dragged on and closed the markets of the Spanish Netherlands and Spanish occupied France to the Merchant Adventurers. After ten boom years, trade was declining and the shrewd Sir Robert struggled hard to diversify especially into shipbuilding, because the number of buccaneers grew. Spanish shipping was preyed upon but English captains suffered losses. Robert now had oversight of Nicholas' old yards on the Thames and Margaret's husband found that close attention had to be given. Rogues were abroad and there was much fraudulent dealing. Robert had to rely on Kit to look after his Exeter interests and he was to discover that this trust was not misplaced.

So Robert did not arrive at High Coombe till late December 1589 and he found the great house wrapped in gloom It was immediately obvious to Robert that Margaret's recovery was slow and he soon discovered why. Margaret had the child at her breast when her husband burst into the great bedchamber. She made no attempt to hand over the little wisp of a babe, whose downy black hair proclaimed its heritage. She raised eyes swimming with tears to meet Robert's enquiring look.

'This is your daughter, Penelope, Robert.'

In fairness to Margaret's kind and loving husband, he had endured a wild voyage, had ridden post-haste up a storm filled valley, through high winds and torrential rain. His dripping beard and cloak bore evidence of this. He was worried about his fortune; he had suffered taunts from his commercial rivals about his landed interests and his new rich wife. The one bright star on the horizon had been his eagerly awaited son. Therefore he could not disguise his disappointment. He gazed at his wife blankly, unable to digest the news. And the silence of the chamber was broken by the noise below of barking dogs, shouting servants and the clatter of horses' hoofs.

'God's truth, wife. Who is calling at this ungodly hour?'

Indeed darkness had set in and it was in the light of flaming torches that Robert saw Elizabeth on her fine mare. Her hair was loose and sparkled with raindrops; her eyes shone and her wide red mouth was smiling. She gestured to her groom, who carried over to her a struggling swaddled child of ten months. Tom Gray's horse was restive and whinnying, back home after a year's absence in Topsham, and the stallion interposed its great body between Robert, standing astride in the doorway, and Elizabeth, who was now clutching her child. Hoarsely, Robert said as he strode forward, 'It's a boy?' and this time Elizabeth dismounted. She pushed back the wet clothes to expose the dark features and black eyes. 'Nicholas Carew Gray,' she cried. 'We call him Carew.'

Now the servants were hastening them indoors out of the rain. Margaret had heard the arrival and thought it was Kit. She had handed her baby back to a wet-nurse who was supplementing her own meagre supply of milk. Then she stood clad in a warm fur-lined bedrobe, at the top of the stairs, looking down at the mêlée of running servants and excited dogs. She marked Tom Gray, but all she could really see was Robert's face, as he cradled a screaming, kicking burden in his arms. It was a face compounded of grief and joy, pride and humility, but above all anger. Perhaps it was in that moment of time that she did not wish to know the truth, for Tom Gray could not see how anyone could mistake Carew for anyone's child but Robert's. Margaret chose to believe that her grandson's precipitate arrival merely heightened Robert's disappointment in his own daughter. Suffice it to say that there was no greater contrast than the mewling, puking Penelope, who wailed day and night, and the vigorous, chubby Carew, who gurgled and kicked in his cradle, throwing off his swaddling clothes and chuckling at everyone who deigned to bend over and to greet him. Margaret soon realised with sorrow that Elizabeth felt nothing for the child, except an overweening pride that she had produced such a handsome, healthy babe. She had handed him to a Flemish wet-nurse at birth and Jeanette was devoted to him, so too was Tom Gray. It was perhaps Tom Gray's love of and devotion to the baby that diverted Margaret's suspicions. She, who had known Tom from early boyhood, should have recognised the young man's capacity for loyalty and love; in the difficult years ahead Tom was as good a father to Carew as any in the land.

Elizabeth would ride out daily, choosing the most mettlesome steed, and indeed these highly bred creatures champed at the bit when they were shut away in their stable and would gallop across the moors with that same fiery spirit which Elizabeth herself displayed. She rode in a fine new wool riding-habit of nut-brown and handsome leather hunting boots. She had a finely chased Flemish saddle and silver harness which jingled as she rode. But she removed the bells when on that frosty January morning she cantered up the valley into the hills towards Bourne.

Robert was seldom to be seen at High Coombe; if he was in the house, he remained in Margaret's chamber where he told his wife he wished to go over estate records. But, on this particular day, Elizabeth, who was ever aware of his presence, had seen him ride out eastwards. The wing of the house set aside for the Grays' use was to the north-east, away from the sight of Foxhole Gap. Indeed it was Beacon Hill which was visible from the windows and reminded Elizabeth constantly of the day on which the Armada was sighted and of her father's part. Carew troubled her not at all, for Margaret insisted that he and Jeanette share

Penelope's nursery, where Alice was so often to be found when she could be spared from the dairy. Anyway Margaret had left her bed when Robert and the Grays returned. She was kept busy with domestic duties now that the household was so enlarged. In the face of Robert's bitter grief and disappointment, she sought to eliminate her own. Penelope was alive and seemed to be gaining strength every day now that Jeanette had charge, and Margaret had given up breast-feeding herself. There would be other children. So Margaret reasoned: meanwhile, in her sympathy and understanding, she was content to let Robert brood alone or to let him lose himself in the business of the estate and of the weaving interests which they had jointly initiated years ago.

So, when Robert rode out towards Bourne he rode alone, and, as on other days, he sat down on a fallen trunk in a clearing and wept alone. He wore long black leather hunting boots; gone was the finery of his London triumphs. Already his dark hair was streaked with grey, his face lined. He held his flat velvet cap in his hands and sat, shoulders bowed, in a veritable arbour of frosty branches and silver cobwebs. He could indeed have been Oberon, mourning for his lost boy, so sylvan was the setting and so fairylike in the glistening silver of hoar frost and pale winter sunlight. Thus Elizabeth chanced upon him, sitting herself astride a grey stallion with a flowing black mane; she too was like a goblin creature, with her dark red hair untrammelled by cap or snood; her pale cream complexion was set off by the rich dark brown of her habit. Her eyes sparkled and her head was held high above that elegant throat and slender body. When Robert looked up, he thought it was some vision of past passion, but it was no idyll, for she said nothing and looked down at him, a scornful smile on her lips. If her eyes gleamed, it was with malice. He said one word, 'Elizabeth.' Slowly she pulled the reins around and, without replying, cantered off up the path. She heard his return to High Coombe later, heard him shouting for her mother and the servants. She could not escape the sound of the flurry of his departure for Exeter: Tom told her that Robert had paid a visit to the nursery and had held both children in his arms. Elizabeth shrugged her shoulders and Tom could not tell what the gesture implied. He suspected that she enjoyed the situation, whereas he feared that at any moment Margaret might discover the truth and everything would come tumbling about their ears.

Tom was therefore immensely relieved when a few days later a messenger came, summoning his foster-mother to Exeter. He saw that Elizabeth was furious, saw it in her flushed cheeks and the rigid stance of her body, the nervous tapping of her feet. She refused to join her husband and her mother at their meal in the Great Hall, pleading that her head ached, so it was Tom and Margaret who discussed the babies' future. 'Penelope will be safe and well here. Robert does not care for her and it is best that she is out of sight. I hate to leave her but no doubt Robert will be shortly to London and that is no place to rear a young child,' said Margaret.

'But, Mother, I myself saw him lift her from her cradle, hold her gently in his arms and allow her to grasp his little finger. He'll come round, you'll see. She is your daughter and he loves you.'

Margaret looked at him with pleading eyes, as if she wanted Tom to repeat the words. She herself said slowly, 'There will be others. He shall have his son.' Briskly, as if she were pushing aside the past and all her melancholy, she continued, 'I hope that your Jeanette will stay. She and Alice are real treasures and your son will do well. What a bonnie lad he is.'

They both smiled. Elizabeth's name was never mentioned: tacitly they recognised that she would not be concerned with the child.

16 The Healing

When Robert arrived in Exeter, he soon found that he was too busy to be weeping and miserable, as he had been at High Coombe. The new house was almost complete and he was anxious to supervise carpenters, stonemasons and plasterers, in order that they would use the most modern designs, such as he had in his London mansion. Then there were City affairs: plans were afoot to put a new front on the Guildhall: as one of Exeter's most prominent citizens, Robert was drawn into the group that financed this latest monument to Exeter's wealth and importance. Always popular, Sir Robert found himself invited to banquets and entertainments, to inspect new wharfs and businesses, to give advice on loans and investments. It all soothed that pride which had been so wounded by the sight of a son whom he could never claim as his own. He began to see that he had been very unfair to Margaret, that she was suffering as much as he from disappointment at Penelope's birth. He was resilient enough to surmount his difficulties and to make sure that Margaret was breeding again.

So, when Margaret arrived on horseback at the city wall, she found her husband and a liveried retinue there to welcome her. The slow procession through Exeter from the east gate was greeted on all sides by tradesmen, who recognised the Penhale heiress and their own City Councillor and newly knighted member

179

of Parliament. Margaret even found gifts pressed into her hand – cheeses, eggs, some finely tanned leather, even a chased silver candlestick. She was touched, as Robert had been, by the warmth of the welcome. It was an auspicious start to a new courtship: Robert installed her in his old lodging, which had been the town house of the Abbots of Tavistock and on which Robert had a long lease, which he could relinquish when 'Rockbeare' was finished. All was ready for her, and Robert insisted that she rest after dinner. She protested, 'I am no longer fragile, my dear.'

His reply, 'But we must safeguard our son's future,' was an indication that, like her, he now looked to the future rather than to the past.

Once again Robert and Margaret invited important citizens, this time of Exeter, to dine and to talk politics and business. They took part in City processions; Margaret was invited to represent Ceres at some local pageant, held to celebrate the anniversary of the building of the bridge over the Exe in 1190. Robert made a jolly Neptune, his increasing girth giving him a faintly bucolic air, in accord with the generous gifts which he, as the god, dispersed amongst the populace. Kit joined them for a time and through him Robert sent to High Coombe a message, which he hid from his wife. The instructions were to Tom Gray to keep Elizabeth away from Exeter and Topsham, and for Tom to help Alice and Tim in caring for Penelope. Margaret seemed content to leave the child where she was, first because of Robert's feelings and secondly because she had discovered that Exeter was not as healthy as she once imagined. An open stream ran down Coombe Street and it was full of stinking odure. Town and country butchers did their slaughtering in the Shambles, and as in London, this proved to be a place where there was stench and flies in the heat of summer. There were fevers and even a case or two of the plague. But Robert would not leave his beloved Rockbeare, which was still not complete: now he was turning attention to the formal gardens and to the furnishings and here Margaret's help was invaluable, as it was in the design and building of extensive storage barns and stables. Margaret longed for the clear reaches of the moors above High Coombe: she missed the woods, although she and Robert would stroll on a summer's evening in the meadows known as Bonhay, which were close to the busy Exe Bridge. She could not have more than one favourite mare with her until the building was complete, so she missed the stud. The leased lodgings were cramped, as Robert had only set up bachelor quarters here; indeed when Kit was in town he stayed elsewhere, but there were plenty of opportunities for him to talk over such matters as estate rents, usury, wool prices and trade in other commodities with his mother.

Margaret's business acumen was respected in Exeter and she could dismiss the fact that she no longer drew men's eyes as she had in London. The swellings in various parts of her body brought on by her last pregnancy were slow to disperse. Plump features were now disfiguring, so that she had a double chin and her fine brown eyes seemed sunk back in her head. Her dark hair was peppered with grey and she had not regained that sprightly and energetic step which had once entranced Robert. They still laughed and teased each other but the lightness of touch was gone: each feared to offend, to bruise damaged and tender feelings. In bed, each strove to reach a pitch of union which would produce an heir, and the striving replaced the ecstasy. They rose weary and unfulfilled. Neither admitted it. Yet still Margaret did not quicken.

As autumn approached, Margaret ventured tentatively to suggest that she might return to High Coombe for harvest celebrations. Almost too eagerly, Robert agreed, explaining that he would go to London and that she could join him later. Margaret hesitated. 'I shall not become pregnant if we part for too long.'

Robert laughed, 'I hope not, my love. I hope not.' She had to be content with that. This time there was no passionate farewell embrace, only a kind of relief on both sides, a respite from the watch which each kept over each other's feelings, words and actions. For the first time in months Margaret slept well. She need no longer be aware of Robert's restless turning and twisting, his sleeping groans, as if he escaped each night into some private purgatory. Now that she could ride out each day, exercise herself and her falcons, now that she could busy herself about the house and yards, Margaret grew prettier. The swellings dispersed. She looked younger, lost her defensive air and surprised herself with singing about the place. Her step was lighter too. She loved her youngest daughter, who seemed to have outgrown her delicacy and was a miniature Robert, sturdy, dark-haired and impossibly energetic, as she tried unsuccessfully to follow Margaret about the house. Carew was always at her side to pick her up and cuddle her when she cried, which she did rarely. He was a delightful little boy, with his mother's charm, but without her petulance. Already he could walk and he would talk gravely in long measured sentences. Penelope would chatter nonsense, incessantly, imitating her mother's tones but not her words, but Carew was silent and unobtrusive, speaking very clearly and carefully when he sensed it to be appropriate. He was by no means solemn, having an enormous sense of fun which delighted the baby Penelope. He adored Jeanette and Tom Gray: he seemed scarcely to notice his mother, on the very few occasions when she appeared. For Elizabeth kept to her wing of the house or else was off to visit neighbours, to hawk, hunt and dance to the early hours. Tom had taken charge of High Coombe once again. The breeding and schooling of horses took up a great deal of his time, as did the supervision of tenant farmers, the collection of rents and the care and supervision of High Coombe's enormous flocks of sheep. Alice and Tim could be relied upon to look after things close to home but abroad it was all in Tom's charge. So he had to be content to see Elizabeth when he could; she was not unkind, but her favours were sparsely distributed. Poor Tom seemed humble and grateful, especially as Elizabeth had kept away from Topsham and Exeter, as he had commanded.

As winter came on, Elizabeth changed. She grew bored and wandered further afield. She took to visiting Kit's house at Topsham, much to his chagrin, and there the young men of Exeter began to congregate, drawn to this new beauty like moths to a flame. For Elizabeth was more beautiful than ever; pregnancy had aged Margaret, it had matured Elizabeth. She had grown taller and her figure was fuller; the waist remained slender as a wand, the arms dimpled and rounded, yet with exquisitely delicate wrists and hands. She was careful to display her equally attractive ankles and tiny feet when she could, feet shod in the latest and prettiest slippers of fine leather and satin. And so Kit found her when he returned in late afternoon from a two-day visit to Falmouth. She was as animated as he had ever seen her, fluttering her dark eyelashes over deep green eyes, whose message each eager follower sought to interpret. The panelled room was dark and the fire low: typically, Elizabeth had forgotten to order the candles lit. Suddenly Kit became aware of Robert at the back of the room and his grim looks surprised Kit, for, in company especially, Robert was renowned for his geniality and humour. It began to dawn on Kit that his sister was putting on a great show. She was enjoying the attention and the flattery and indeed her lissom figure and cream complexion were shown to perfection in peach brocade

with an orange overskirt and finely embroidered
stomacher. The tiny jewelled cap set off her chestnut
hair. Even in the twilight of a winter's afternoon, Kit
could see how she glanced mischievously under heavy
lids to see what effect she was having on the glowering
Robert. Kit was very fond of Tom Gray and wondered
how he coped with Elizabeth's many extravagances. His
silent reverie was broken when Robert strode over to
him and whispered, 'Send this lot packing. They have
better things to do than listen to that young chit's
gossip.'

True it was that Elizabeth was lightly touching upon
the idle vanities and foibles of her neighbours. It was
not for the first time that Robert noticed how like Letitia
Elizabeth had grown in looks and manners. He
remembered his old friend Nicholas with regret,
recalling how proud he had been of this little minx.
Robert's own feelings were compounded of jealousy,
anger and frustration. He pulled himself up, aware that
Kit was very shrewd and that he must gain no inkling of
the true state of affairs. In fact Kit's suspicions grew.

Kit had always disliked his sister and now he began to
hate her. At eighteen years of age he was still too young
to appreciate how desperately unhappy she was and
how she sought to divert herself from that misery. She
neglected her husband and her son and Kit envied her
this child, for he longed for a family of his own. When
Elizabeth rode about the county making a name for
herself as a silly flirt, Kit remembered his father's old
mistress Letitia and her stupid heartless conduct. Kit
was sick at heart. He had been worried about his mother
since Penelope's birth and just recently had been
heartened to see some recovery. But he wondered at
Robert's presence in Topsham, because his mother had
believed her husband already departed for London.

Once Elizabeth had left for High Coombe, albeit
reluctantly, and only when Kit had seen her suitably

escorted, Robert clarified the position. 'I had meant to depart for London ere now, but trouble at the Cornish panneries delayed me. I am resolved to fetch your mother before I take ship.'

Robert was amused, with a sick humour, for it was not until he had seen Elizabeth once again that he had resolved to protect himself with Margaret's presence. Anger filled him and it could only be assuaged with a legitimate male heir. He was glad that Kit could not read his thoughts, altho' that night they sat over the fire, companionably discussing national affairs and Exeter business gossip. Next morning he rode to High Coombe to find his wife deep in housewifely tasks of preserving and boiling. She was flushed from exertion and heat, but somehow he found the domestic scene curiously reassuring, more so when he espied a pretty little rogue at her skirts, smiling and chattering nonsense. 'Can this be Penelope?' he cried, as he lifted her high above the stone-flagged floor. All the servants gathered round and gaped. It was kitchen gossip that the new master cared nought for his daughter. The centre of attention, Penelope responded with laughter and eager cries. Margaret could not help a secret prayer that Carew would not appear on the scene. But all was well as Tom had carried the boy off to see a newborn foal and had not been able to drag Penelope away from her mother.

'Let us all go to London,' Robert cried.

'Penelope as well?' queried Margaret.

'Of course. She is our own Robin Goodfellow. She will bring us luck.' He smiled at his wife over the child's dark head.

From that moment, Robert grew as devoted to his jolly daughter as she to him. In London she thrived and her father believed that he had forgotten Elizabeth and her son.

17   Re-enter Letitia

Elizabeth did not forget Robert. She had stayed in her room and sulked after her precipitate return from Topsham. She was therefore surprised to descend after two days to find her mother and Penelope just departed for London, in Robert's company. She was more angry and frustrated than ever and Tom Gray's patience was sorely tried. Now she gave way to violent temper tantrums, not just with Tom himself but with friends and neighbours, so that she became the subject of gossip and enormous embarrassment to her family. She would round on a guest for some innocent words and shout vicious remarks about their views or their family. On the last occasion, Kit had come with a friend who was also a partner in a new trading venture. To the horror of the reserved and proud Kit, Elizabeth turned on his guest. 'How can you say that the Queen is the heart and soul of this country? She is a sick old woman, nothing more.' It was sacrilege, if not treason, and Nicholas Trenow must have turned in his grave. Kit got up from the table where they were dining and seized his sister by the shoulders, 'Lizzie, forbear. Forbear. This is dangerous talk. You can disgrace the family.' It was the worst thing that he could have said and Tom, who sat helpless at the head of the table, knew it. For at that moment, Elizabeth hated them all, Trenows, Bournes, Penhales and most of all the Fursdons. So he rose and, in a quiet tone, said, 'Elizabeth, you are needed in the kitchens.'

His wife laughed. 'I am never needed, Tom. Do not try to cozen me because I embarrass you.' She laughed again, a wild laugh. 'You, who are the son of a peasant, to be humiliated. If you are at the bottom, you can't get any lower, can you?'

Tom flushed and said nothing. The two observers had seen enough and rose abruptly from the table; Kit was thankful that he could rely on Edward's discretion not to discuss his sister's folly. They left the house immediately; now, once again, Tom faced a tirade. Elizabeth shouted and stormed; she even tried to strike her husband, but he was too quick for her and carried her off to the privacy of the east wing, where eventually her cries and sobs subsided and she sank into a restless sleep. Tom sat in a chair, eyes wide open. Next day he resolved to act, for he found a pale and wild-looking Elizabeth mounting her son on a large and unsuitable pony, prepared to trot off to the moors. 'That pony is too big for him, Elizabeth.' Carew was fearless, already had a good seat and sat boldly astride, clasping the reins tightly. Undoubtedly however his mount was too strong for him to control. He howled when Tom seized him from behind and Elizabeth, hovering above her husband on her mettlesome grey stallion, hissed venomously, 'Leave my son alone.' In one movement Tom had thrown the screaming child into the arms of Jeanette, who had stood close by, watching her mistress in alarm. Tom commanded her to take the boy back to the nursery. Now Elizabeth raised her crop and brought it down, murderously, across Tom's shoulders. 'How dare you,' she cried. 'He is mine and I will do what I will.' Since the whole scene was enacted in the stable-yard at High Coombe, servants had run to the doorways, not so much because of their mistress's screams, as because the stallion was leaping, pounding the cobblestones and whinnying, the highly-bred creature infected by his rider's hysteria. Nearby the mares in their stalls were responding, with the high-pitched cry of female to male, in excitement and distress. With enormous courage, Tom seized the bridle and was in great danger from the prancing hoofs. Elizabeth continued to strike out at Tom and drew blood with a slap across his forehead. Although the grooms, who had now come out of the stables, recognised their mistress's equestrian skills, they were concerned for her horse and rushed to relieve Tom. Suddenly aware of her audience, humiliated beyond reason, Elizabeth slid from the saddle and ran indoors. Tom knew that she was after Carew and he pursued her, only to find that Jeanette had wisely slipped away with her charge and could not be found. Now Tom and Elizabeth faced each other in the nursery, and Tom was suddenly aware that Elizabeth looked ill. She was very thin and her white skin was drawn like parchment across the fine bones. The deep green eyes were wild and sunk deep in her skull. He began to fear for her reason. He always forgot that his wife was ever mindful of her own welfare and would draw back just as her body rebelled against the violence of her moods. As if the scene below had never been enacted, she said carelessly, throwing her fine feathered cap onto a nearby chest, 'I need a change. I shall go to Yealmpton.'

Tom's first thoughts were of relief, for above all he worried about Carew. The little boy had taken Penelope's departure hard, and he had begun to pine for her. As he grew older, his mother's sudden interest in him, interspersed as it was with long bouts of indifference, bewildered him further. So Tom longed for Elizabeth to put distance between herself and the child. Then a suspicion dawned. Was it her intention to pursue Robert to London? Indeed a plan was already forming at the back of Elizabeth's mind, but for the moment she did want to see Letitia to enlist her sympathy. The latest humiliation had bitten deep.

* * *

The Lady Letitia still endeavoured to preserve her youthful charms. Like the old Queen, she wore wigs. Hers was black and accentuated the heavily powdered white face, where the wrinkles could not be hidden. Letitia did not reveal her body to her fifth husband, Roger Blyth, but embraced him in the darkness of her great bed. He was the only one to bring her no fortune, but he was young, handsome and lusty. One late winter's afternoon, she was therefore a little dismayed when the very youthful and very beautiful Elizabeth rode in, closely escorted by her mother's henchman, Luke, for Tom Gray took no chances on his wife's desire to escape to London. He understood that she was frustrated in love.

Elizabeth's frenetic activities and her many flirtations, which had drawn her time and time again to the very brink of taking a lover, were attempts to hide from herself the mixed love, hate and resentment which she had for Robert. She failed to realise that, for her, Robert had always been the father substitute for the one who was so often absent from her life. Nicholas' death had left such a gap and Robert's skilful lovemaking had awoken her sensuality. To some extent, Tom satisfied her; she adored his fidelity, whilst scorning his dog-like submission. A little more spirit would have brought her more often to his bed. But, above all, her overweening vanity was hurt. From childhood, she had taken her beauty for granted, and she had found that it helped her to get what she wanted. She knew that it did not work on her mother and she sensed her mother's jealousy of the attention which Nicholas lavished on her, a jealousy which Margaret had never acknowledged. Elizabeth despised her mother's plain looks and her inability to make herself attractive to men. Unconsciously, from an early age she determined that she would

never be like that and that she would never allow her
husband or her lovers to neglect her, as Nicholas had
neglected Margaret. It was gall that this plain, dumpy
little woman should have captured the love of her life.
For, deprived of him, rejected by him, this is how she
now saw Robert, just as she saw Margaret as a dowdy old
lady, when in fact Margaret had always been handsome,
dignified and attractive. Like her father, Elizabeth was
given over to fantasies and to wanting always what she
could not have.

The visit to Letitia was a ploy, a means to get to
London, to plague Robert yet again, so, for once, she
ignored the attentions of Letitia's latest husband and
made it clear that she was Letty's friend.

Angry at so blatant a rejection, Roger Blyth went off
to Plymouth in a huff, to amuse himself in the dockside
stews and taverns, in which the port abounded. Letitia
was pleased because Roger already bored her and she
was intrigued by Elizabeth's air of mystery. The girl was
obviously dying to take her into her confidence; but
Elizabeth was astute. She knew Letitia for an inveterate
gossip, so although she told her about her lusty lover,
she did not reveal his identity. Her picture of Tom Gray
and the quarrel hardly accorded with her sturdy, steady
husband and his rock-like loyalty, but Letitia neither
knew nor cared. She did know how much Elizabeth
disliked her mother and this amused her, for it
reminded her of Nicholas Trenow, whose devotion was
now enshrined in her memory. But she did not see why
she should provide Elizabeth with a cover for going to
London to meet her lover.

'It is all so boring now. The Queen is aged and the
young men all pretend to be in love with the old
harridan. She won't have pretty girls around, and she
won't have dancing. Really, Elizabeth, I don't want to go
and in winter too.'

'But we shall have fun, Letty. You have a London

house and we can entertain. Do you remember winter parties in the snow?' Letitia remained adamant.

But Roger returned from Plymouth and added his pleas to Elizabeth's. They both flattered her. Letitia was vain and stupid, even Nicholas had finally recognised that. Above all she was very tired and these two young people wore her down, so she gave in. Once they were on their way to the capital, her two companions almost forgot her. Elizabeth began to flirt with Roger and he responded to the advances of a beautiful young girl, who was such a contrast to his ageing and demanding old wife. Letitia was jolted over roads rutted with hard frost in a cold and evil-smelling carriage. She never had cared much for horses and now her stiffening joints prevented her from riding at all. Meanwhile her husband and friend rode ahead, laughing and joking, obviously invigorated by the crisp clear air. Even the dirty flea-ridden inns could not dampen their enthusiasm. Roger loved to talk to the strange characters, who were pleased to share a flagon with him and, tedium at last relieved, Elizabeth threw off her melancholy and won the admiration of every man they chanced upon. She began to allow Roger liberties that she had allowed no others, saving her husband. It was a poor return for Letitia's kindness and guidance in the past. Unconsciously, Elizabeth's own self-esteem was enhanced by the company of this sophisticated but ageing beauty. Elizabeth remembered her father's devotion to this woman and secretly laughed at her attempts to beautify herself, to pad out the scrawny figure and to disguise the rounded shoulders. When Robert saw her again for the first time, it was just as she had hoped. He saw her against the backcloth of Letitia's age and Letitia's husband. For by the time they reached London, Roger was quite lovelorn and made no attempt to hide it. Elizabeth was at the very pinnacle of her beauty, dressed in the height of fashion. Vivacious, charming and sophisticated, she was no longer the innocent young girl who had bewitched the susceptible Robert, but someone infinitely more fascinating and desirable. So Elizabeth played the 'hard to catch' game. She saw her ex-lover only in company. She hunted in the villages around London with some of his older friends, but she was still escorted by the ubiquitous Roger. She attended great City functions, cynosure of all eyes, her delicate features and brilliant colouring set off by gowns of deep sapphire, amber, russet and even black. Elizabeth had an instinct for clothes, for settings, for activities which showed her to advantage. She was obsessed, not with Robert, but with the chase. She was the huntress, Diana, but also the hunted. This time she need resort to no love philtres; she left that to Letitia.

Then, suddenly, within a year of her arrival in London, Letitia died of a mysterious wasting disease, which left her gasping for breath, unable to eat or drink. It was an horrific end. Roger, who was an ill-born and shallow young man, inherited all her fortune and seemed set to lavish it upon Elizabeth.

* * *

Margaret had been horrified when her daughter arrived in London, in the company of Lady Letitia. Margaret looked in vain to Tom Gray. Yet she could not bring herself to invite Elizabeth to stay with them. Robert seemed uneasy in her presence and she put this down to a fear that Elizabeth's tempestuous nature might lead to a social gaffe. Since the bestowal of his knighthood, Robert's consciousness of his own position as a 'parvenue' made him sensitive to any deviation from the most strict etiquette and protocol. It was the only area where he might perhaps have been dubbed old-fashioned, as he could not do with the more relaxed manners of the young. He was never bored by the Court but found the slow pace and rigid ceremonial both reassuring and satisfying. Margaret was not invited because most women, other than the Queen's own ladies, were banned; it did not trouble her. She could still accompany Robert to all the great ceremonies of the City and the livery companies: sometimes she would see Elizabeth in the distance. She too noted the presence of Roger Blyth: she did not like the young man. But Margaret was sensible and thought that she knew her daughter. A married man was a more suitable escort for Tom's wife than some unattached young sprig. When she asked Robert his opinion, he muttered something about the youth's stupidity, but otherwise could not be drawn. There were occasions when Margaret wasn't present when Elizabeth drew Robert's eyes.

For Margaret and her husband had settled back into a comfortable companionship, much like the early days of their friendship. Robert seemed reconciled to his wife's continuing barren and thus to Penelope as his heiress, for the girl flourished, growing daily more like her father. He loved her sturdy courage, her inveterate good humour; nothing daunted her. The house rang with her laughter. She soon began to talk and reveal a quick intelligence and a sharp eye. How loath Margaret was to reintroduce that restless spirit which was Elizabeth Gray back into her serene and ordered household. She believed that she had no choice when Letitia died. It was obvious to everyone that Roger was enslaved by Elizabeth's charms. He might, for the moment, be engrossed in lawyers' wrangles over settlements, lands, loans, rents and ventures which Letitia had inherited from her four husbands. He must pretend to a semblance of mourning, but obviously the removal of the restraint of Letitia's presence must present a threat to Elizabeth, a fact which she herself recognised.

Yet it was with an ill grace that Margaret's daughter

received her mother and allowed her escort to Robert's house on the Thames, which she, Nicholas and Robert had planned when Elizabeth was a young girl. She had not seen the building and garden completed. Sight of it fuelled the unreasonable anger which boiled in her at the sight of her mother. Letitia's London house had been modest by contrast, her houses small in relation to her fortune. The grandeur of the building, the enormous rooms and high gilded, plastered ceilings, the rich wainscots, the vast fireplaces, all ablaze with great fires and expensive wax candles, together with a multitude of servants, astounded Elizabeth. She saw Robert descend the great wide staircase with its carved newel posts, cross the vast tiled hall, hung with pictures and tapestries. Gravely, he bid her welcome and was immediately repelled by the spite in her tone. 'I find my lady mother fatigued by her care for my comfort and reputation. I would surmise that she needs rest.'

Margaret and Robert knew that she was referring obliquely and scornfully to her mother's appearance, and husband and wife smiled at each other, conspiratorially. Margaret sighed. The unease was back, even as Elizabeth crossed the threshold. The appearance of a chattering Penelope did not relieve the tension, for her half-sister had no patience with the little girl, and the child was taken aback, for she had grown to expect all their visitors to greet her with warmth and affection. His daughter's confusion riled Robert, for he well understood what lay behind Elizabeth's cool manner. He thought, 'Damn the girl, the sooner she returns to High Coombe the better.' Yet his pulse quickened, his whole body alert to her presence, and when he looked into her eyes he knew that she had sensed his reaction. Once more, Elizabeth smiled, the sensuous, lingering, hungry look of yore.

18   The Affair

It was sad to reflect that no-one, especially Margaret, would ever know how hard Robert fought to resist Elizabeth's challenge. Every instinct marshalled itself against every move of the senses. He knew that she was evil, that to succumb to her wiles was to court disaster. But Elizabeth used every weapon – her beauty, her charm and above all her youth. What man growing older has not felt himself hold back the flood of time in the arms of a younger woman, has not experienced the triumph of renewing his sexual vigour at the temple of youth itself! But Robert did hold out. She wheedled and cajoled, assuring him that she merely wanted a meeting to talk over old times. If Margaret noticed the girl engaging her husband in earnest talk, it was an assurance to her that Robert and Elizabeth were friends again. Then Elizabeth threatened to tell Margaret everything, unless her stepfather agreed to a secret tryst alone with her, at a secluded inn in the outlying village of Chelsea.

As he rode out one morning, Robert tried to recall his wife, her serenity and her patience, but all he could do was feel an ache in the groin and a great sense of well-being, so that the glorious summer morning, full of birdsong and sunlight, seemed to conspire against his loyalty and good sense. Elizabeth refused to talk outside the inn. 'We shall be seen,' she said, although, in fact, she was long past caring about public opinion or indeed about anything except the gratification of her own needs. With mounting excitement, she followed Robert and the inn-servant upstairs to a small, dark, hot chamber, where even the wide-flung windows could not let in enough air, but where the hum of bees in the lavender hedge below matched the buzzing of flies under the low ceiling. An enormous four-poster took up all the space and, as Robert dismissed the serving man, Elizabeth sat demurely on the bed tucking up her legs. Robert bent low in the doorway and, suddenly, flung himself upon her, almost sobbing. He tore the jewelled cap off her head with such force that her eyes watered from the hairpins inadvertently pulled out. Then her lover sunk his own head in her bosom. His wet red lips found the large roseate nipples erect and inviting. He ripped open his points and lifted her skirts. Gone was all that finesse which he had employed with Margaret. But the girl in front of him responded with vigour to what might have seemed an attempt at rape. They rolled over and over across the great bed, crying aloud each other's names. Now it was begun: Robert could not finish it. He rode as often as he could to the same trysting place, there to find her, ready and waiting.

Margaret was used to his absences on business and her daughter kept so often to her room that Margaret never knew whether Elizabeth was home or abroad. But gradually she became conscious of Elizabeth's soft looks and quiet demeanour. In company, she was almost demure; gone were the tempers and the pouting sulks. Even the malice was absent. Margaret's heart bled for dear faithful Tom Gray, who was busy looking after her beloved High Coombe, for her daughter surely had found a lover and Margaret suspected that it was not the callow youth, Roger Blyth, who still hung around the place. Should she inform her son-in-law and allow him to discover the culprit? Should she let the affair run its course? The months went by. Elizabeth was obviously head over heels in love: the dark rings under her eyes, the languor of her movements and the uncharacteristic kindness of her manners towards family and servants all alarmed and alerted her mother. Once again, Robert was little help and only muttered about a young girl's follies, before changing the subject. Margaret gave no hint that she was taking the drastic step of ordering her son-in-law to join them; she decided to take action before winter set in and journeying became difficult. She hoped that Tom would bring Carew and, with desperation, trusted that, by his very presence, her son would indicate to Elizabeth the folly of her ways. For knowing Elizabeth's impetuosity, Margaret feared that her daughter would run off with her lover and ruin her reputation for ever.

When Tom Gray arrived with Carew in the early winter of 1592 he caught a secret glance between Robert and Elizabeth, which his foster-mother missed, because she was hugging her three-year-old grandson; this glance was compounded of alarm, and apprehension, with an infuriating hint of amusement.

Tom had fretted away the months and years of Elizabeth's absence. With dismay he heard of the journey to London and the subsequent death of the Lady Letitia, guessing that Margaret would insist on her daughter joining Robert's household. Margaret's letters described the new quieter Elizabeth and perturbed him further. Tom was angry to think that these two lovers could betray both their partners, after his care and concern for the child and for Elizabeth's good name. He wanted to believe that Elizabeth was disillusioned with Robert, that her flirtations revealed a frivolous nature. He did not want to see her as the faithless and self-centred creature that she was. That scene in the great chamber of Robert's London house was etched in his memory for ever. His first sight of the brilliant young woman, glowing with health, eyes sparkling, her whole body alive with love, convinced him of her guilt. Robert's secret and silent communication with her confirmed his fears. He looked away, keeping his own eyes on the ground, apparently distracted by the children.

Margaret was relieved to find that the boy, Carew, no longer disturbed her husband. He merely laughed at the antics of Penelope who would tease her companion, pull his black hair and run away to hide in the house, which she knew so well and which was new to him. Yet she was compassionate too and hugged him when one of Robert's mastiffs knocked him over and banged his head against a chest. Then too they were often to be found in the stables, feeding the ponies titbits, for they both loved horses. They could both ride and were allowed out into Temple Fields away behind the Inns of Court. They would run races and make their mounts jump over logs, placed deliberately in their rides. Since they were barely three years old – the sturdy Penelope, big for her age, had not yet reached her third birthday – their riding feats were the pride of the household and that included Robert. A hard and demanding life had made it possible for Margaret's husband to hide his feelings beneath a bluff and genial exterior, so that even she could not guess at the conflicting passions which tore him apart. Robert conjectured that Tom Gray was suspicious and knew that he, together with Tom's wife, must be circumspect above all things. But Elizabeth was at her old game, learnt from Letitia, of playing one against another. She began to encourage Roger Blyth again and this infuriated Tom, who correctly saw the flirtations as a front and a torment. Robert was too besotted to recognise his mistress' duplicity. It was he, who, one afternoon in Temple Fields, watching the children's equestrian games, got close enough to Elizabeth to whisper the need for a further assignation at the Chelsea tavern. He could not tell her that he had asked Tom to go to Kit's shipyards at Deptford, but Tom too had learnt duplicity in a hard school. He sent Luke on his behalf.

Tom hid in a lane close by Margaret's house and watched Elizabeth emerge to lose herself in the thick crowds. He wondered at her tenacity in riding alone in streets through a mêlée of rogues and vagabonds who solicited alms, as well as throngs of finely dressed gentlemen and merchants, themselves throwing admiring glances at the handsomely dressed young woman. Tom reasoned that the stench of open drains and unwashed bodies must offend his fastidious wife, who would only ride through the farmyards at High Coombe with a pomander to her nose. Tom was amused and repelled by the antics of some tiny dwarfs, who were entertaining a crowd of buxom women up from the country to sell their cheese, butter and eggs. He saw a pick-pocket at work amongst them. All these trivial details registered with him, whilst he kept Elizabeth's fine grey feathered hat in sight as it bobbed in and out, and she cantered onwards. Tom became aware that he was sweating heavily, despite the wintry weather, for even whilst he laughed at the crowds, he was stroking a poniard, which he had stuck in his belt. Anger and frustration made his head pound. He was certain that Elizabeth was on her way to meet Robert but, with all his heart, he prayed that it was not so. If she had an engagement with poor silly Roger or any other frivolous young blade, he could endure it, but if she betrayed him with her mother's husband, he could not. Black jealousy tortured him but so did a rush of overwhelming pity for the innocent lady who had mothered him from a small boy. He loved Margaret, but he also admired her; for her generosity, for her courtesy to her inferiors and for her loving kindness. Perhaps Tom's passion was fuelled by a secret fear that

he had played a part in the betrayal of the Lady
Margaret.

Now Tom was no longer conscious of his surroundings; he rode at a discreet distance, as the crowd
thinned. As she rode through the woods, he kept his
wife's grey mare in sight, but was himself hidden
amongst the trees. He pulled up his own mount in order
that he could observe Elizabeth. He noted with pleasure
that the inn-yard was crowded and noisy, busy with the
comings and goings of travellers, the ring of horses'
hooves on the cobbles, the shouted orders to ostlers and
pot-boys. He was careful to hitch his horse at some
distance from the inn; an unprepossessing nag, it was
unlikely to be stolen. His patience was rewarded: fifteen
minutes later Robert rode into the inn-yard. Tom drew
himself into a long dark cloak, hiding his face, and
strode purposefully after his quarry. Now he hesitated
behind the great oak door, beyond which he could hear
Robert's bellowing laughter and Elizabeth's lighter
tones. Was the door barred? And then suddenly Robert
opened it and called out an order for a flagon of ale;
Tom had scarcely a minute to whisk himself behind the
dusty arras which was at the top of the stairs. He waited
and no-once came, not surprising, as the tavern servants
were fully occupied. When Tom flung wide the door,
Robert obviously thought that it was the pot-boy and
remained behind the bed-curtains, saying, 'Leave it
there, lad. I'll see you later.' Trembling with rage, Tom
shut the door and shot the bolt across. The couple in the
bed had heard the noise and there was a sudden silence.
As Tom opened the thick curtains, which he noticed
were red, it was to see Elizabeth's face beneath Robert's
great bulk. Her look changed from amazement to
horror, her eyes opened wide and she flung her arms
upward, almost in supplication; as she did so, Robert
half-turned his body to face the intruder. Tom had
been a seaman, had fought for his life amongst hostile

Spaniards; he knew just where to place the dagger and plunged it as hard as he could with two hands into Robert's chest above the heart and then withdrew it. Blood spurted everywhere and Robert's body sank on to the bed and then slid slowly to the floor. Elizabeth began to scream; with great presence of mind, Tom closed the bed-curtains. As he hoped, the inn sounds of horses' hooves and travellers' orders, the bawdy laughter and the rolling of heavy barrels, deadened the noise from above and Tom was able to flee, unobserved, at speed, down the staircase and across the yard to his impatient horse.

Elizabeth could never remember the events that followed. She was conscious only that she must get help for Robert. The innkeeper wanted no trouble; he was certain that the man was dead, but he bundled the gentleman, wrapped in the crimson bed-curtains, and the half-naked distraught young woman into one of the farm-carts parked at the rear. Elizabeth gave her bewildered driver instructions to reach Robert's house. It grew dark and the bony and ancient nag which was drawing the farm-cart grew slower and slower as it approached London. Still Elizabeth hung over Robert, stroking his head and whispering endearments. As they rode into the yard, the servants ran out with flaming torches to view the half-fainting, bloodstained young woman with horror. It was generally assumed that they had been attacked by footpads. No-one questioned their return together. Margaret was too shocked at the sight to register any query. It was Luke, newly returned from Deptford, who mounted the cart and saw the still body, wrapped in its crimson cloak. He wanted to forestall Margaret, but saw her white face loom next to his own. she said quietly, 'Carry Mistress Gray indoors and to her room, Luke, I will see to this.'

Margaret did not faint when they laid Robert's body on the bed and she saw the torn shirt and the bloody, gaping wound. His black eyes stared up at her and his mouth was distorted in a hideous rictus of agony. She heard the servants' talk of footpads, allowed the major-domo to summon the watch; she knew it was to no avail.

For Luke came and told her that he could get no sense out of her daughter. Whilst Margaret commanded the household, instructed Jeanette to keep the children away at all costs, whilst she rewarded the inn-driver and asked him to send the couple's horses back on the morrow, she kept her thoughts at bay. Somewhere they were racing around like ants burrowing away in her brain, but she refused to let them out until Luke came again with troubled face, to tell her that she must hasten at once to Elizabeth's room. The apothecary had come and bled the girl but she lay unconscious, tossing and turning in a high fever. Suddenly she started to shout out and Luke began to distinguish a few words. So Margaret came in and sent away the timid maid who had stripped off the girl's bloodstained garments, and sponged her fevered face and body. Only Luke was there and he was commanded to the door.

All through the night, Margaret heard her daughter's ravings. Robert's name was repeated again and again, interspersed with endearments and beseechings. The girl cried aloud in an ecstasy of passion; she yelled at Tom to let her lover go. Margaret's thoughts could no longer be held back. She gazed down at this daughter, whom she had never truly loved and who had betrayed her so hideously. She bathed her forehead, straightened her tortured limbs, held a soothing and quietening posset of poppy juice to her lips. All the time she was screaming silently, 'No, Robert. No. You are not capable of such treachery. Not you.' But no word passed her lips, other than instructions to Luke that Kit must be summoned from Topsham.

19 Aftermath

There was no way by which Kit could reach Margaret's side in time for Robert's funeral. It was possible because of winter weather to delay the burial but that same weather held Kit in port for several days after the frantic messenger arrived. Servants whispered in corners about the mysterious absence of Tom Gray, but no-one, except Margaret and Luke, attended upon Elizabeth. It became obvious to Robert's friends and acquaintances that someone had to take charge and an informal meeting of his livery company led to plans for a grand funeral, in which Robert's wife played little part. When she emerged from Elizabeth's chamber on a cold February morning, she discovered an escort of finely accoutred gentlemen to hand.

Robert would have loved the pageantry and ceremonial. The coffin was carried in front of his magnificent black stallion, which was in full harness with a poignant empty saddle. The members of the City Council and the Lord Mayor, together with representatives of the guilds and their banners, followed behind in solemn procession. Margaret chose to ride her mare, for she could not bear the close confinement of her clumsy carriage. In the absence of other members of the family, she was escorted by members of Robert's household, some of whom began to weep, even before they left the courtyard. And this was the mood of the day, for it rained a steady drizzle and soon there was more weeping because Robert was very popular and would be sorely missed. The religious service was solemn but uplifting; in a tiny corner of her mind Margaret appreciated the fine music, but she doubted that Robert would have done. She thought that he would have appreciated more the heraldic devices and accoutrements of a knight of the realm, which adorned the coffin.

Otherwise, for Margaret, dry-eyed, the day went by in a hazy dream; by the time her guests arrived back at the mansion to a feast organised by the major-domo, the gargantuan quantities of meat and fish, accompanied by elaborate confections of every description, together with cider, ale and wine, caused Margaret to retch, so that she fled for a few minutes to the closeness of her bedchamber, now empty for the first time since the return of her husband's body. When she descended again, dusk was already setting in and a multitude of candles had to be lit in the Great Hall and the blaze, mingling with the last remains of daylight, together with the leaping flames of two great fires, led to the dance of grotesque shadows on the walls, those same shadows chasing each other in and out of the plastered devices, and gilded ceilings, the brilliant colours of which were subdued by the weird combinations of light and shadow. Somehow they seemed to be torturing Margaret and to reflect her own black and evil thoughts which she was trying unsuccessfully to subdue. All this Margaret noticed through the fog which separated her from the glittering and grandiloquent throng of friends and neighbours. She also observed a solemn Penelope, clad magnificently in a miniature gown like her mother's; and Carew, brought forth to bow to the assembled company as a mark of gratitude to those who had gathered in Robert's honour. Many a merchant looked with a greedy eye upon the sturdy figure of the little girl, who was now one of the wealthiest heiresses in London, if not in the kingdom.

Robert, with typical optimism, had reckoned to outlive

Margaret and had willed both their fortunes to the heirs of his body, of whom there was only one legitimate person, namely Penelope Penhale Fursdon. Kit was the guardian and trustee and when he rode in, exhausted, two weeks after the funeral, his first call was upon his two wards, for it was obvious that Carew was his responsibility too. Kit had been made aware of his sister's mental condition and he had learnt of Tom Gray's continuing absence. Before the fire, in the privacy of his mother's bedchamber, she poured out the whole sordid story, which he had begun to piece together earlier on his voyage from the West. Only now could Margaret reveal her terrible suspicion, opened up by Tom's absence and confirmed by Elizabeth's wild words, that he had murdered Robert. Kit had already guessed as much. Now Margaret wept for the first time since Robert's death. She knelt at Kit's feet and her tears flowed so copiously that her son began to fear that she would never stop. Yet he knew his mother well, her strength and her wisdom. Like him, her concern was all for the children, to prevent any scandal or gossip. So finally she dried her eyes, rose to her feet like some very old woman and sent Kit on his way with a silent embrace.

Within a month Elizabeth was dead and her mother and brother felt an enormous relief, for neither of them could see how they might forestall any sudden outburst or revelation on the part of the deranged young woman. She could be confined as a lunatic, but Margaret shuddered at the prospect, for she believed that Elizabeth would regain her senses. It did not happen because Elizabeth's body was found floating in the Thames at the bottom of the garden. It had been Luke's turn to watch the prisoner and he had not only slept, but also failed to bar the door. In the morning he woke to find her gone. When the body was found a solemn Kit summoned the old man, and they stood one at each end of the private parlour, which Kit had set aside for his use. From the window-seat, his back turned to the servant, Kit said, 'You are a faithful servitor, Luke. We are all in God's hands.' Luke said nothing; he stared down at his feet and shifted in embarrassment. The sound of children's laughter drifted in from the garden, where the first signs of spring were just appearing.

Despite the ebullience of the children, it was a sad, slow procession which, in the spring of 1593, wound its way across the country to High Coombe. It was obvious to them all that Margaret was a sick woman; she told no-one of the small lump in her breast, which grew daily but gave her no more than a feeling of discomfort. The canker that gnawed within her was one of guilt, that she had secretly rejoiced at Elizabeth's death, that she had neglected her daughter all her life. Margaret knew that Nicholas, then Robert, had always had first place. Then there was the management of affairs at High Coombe, the stud and the great flocks. Ambition had led her into weaving and into trade and shipbuilding. She scarcely knew her children, Alice and Tim as well as Elizabeth, saving only Kit who had been her constant companion. 'I have never been a mother,' she mourned to herself. 'Old Sally gave more to my babies than I did.' Then a little voice whispered, 'You cossetted John.' But John had died, possibly because Elizabeth was jealous and that was her mother's fault too. Slow mile by slow mile, Margaret castigated herself, to arrive at each dreary tavern more exhausted than the day before. Kit supervised the lumbering wagons, which carried Robert's magnificent furnishings and all his goods down to the West, to High Coombe and Exeter. Margaret had been adamant that the London house must be cleared and shut up. She knew that she would never return and it would be long years before Penelope was ready to make her home there. Margaret's love for High

Coombe was the one rock to cling to at this time. She felt
that only there might she recover, amongst her beloved
woods and hills, deep in her Devon countryside which
she loved so dearly. Meanwhile Kit had also to look to
Jeanette and the children. Although he was completely
unaware of it, the faithful nurse was more than a little in
love with her handsome new employer. But the
expression of that emotion was in unfailing devotion to
his two wards, whom she kept happy and amused in the
tedious hours of that slow journey. Penelope missed her
jolly father and the fun of her life in London, but she
had Jeanette and Carew. She sensed her mother's
unhappiness, but she was kept away from her. Kit was a
new and exciting person in her life, who, although he
did not joke or tease like her father, would come every
night to talk to the children about the wonders of the
journey – the patient oxen whom they had seen at the
plough, the baby rabbits who ran startled across their
path, the great lumbering carriages of the rich who
passed them in the opposite direction on their way to
London. Kit had tales of the boar, the phoenix, the
dragon – or the curly-tailed lions which adorned the
doors of those same carriages. The laughing serving-
maids and their incomprehensible jokes intrigued
Penelope and Carew. The boy did not reveal to anyone
how much he missed Tom. Everyone knew that Robert
was dead, but Tom Gray's absence was ignored. Carew
had learnt early to hide his feelings; his mother's
behaviour had always bewildered him and made him
cautious about showing his emotions. Gradually, Kit
would learn that Carew was much like himself. At this
moment of time, Kit was content to love the children;
understanding came later.

The biggest compensation for the children was arrival
at High Coombe. Carew had some vague memories of
its wonders, Penelope had none. All the servants were
gathered to greet them, faces full of sympathy for the

mistress and joy at the bouncing vigour of the children. Now Penelope and Carew met the diminutive Alice, who initiated them into the mysteries of the milking parlour and the dairy. Tim allowed them to learn the names of all the cows. They could not have arrived at a better time, for everywhere there were young creatures, chicks, ducklings, goslings, calves, lambs and above all foals. Up in the woods, they could espy the delicate shy deer with their fawns. Altogether it was one great delight. Robert and Tom faded in their memories, even Margaret. For she was now so sick that she rarely left her chamber.

20 The Witch

An uneasy calm settled over the household. Everyone went quietly about their business, as summer came in with hazy sunshine, early morning mists and brilliant afternoons. The edge of the woods and the borders of the lanes were full of wild flowers, huge golden kingcups, ox-eye daisies, ragwort, speedwell and wild roses. Penelope and Carew would gather great armfuls and carry them to Margaret's chamber where the sick woman, often in great pain, would lift herself to greet them with a pale smile. Just as she had extended her love to Nicholas' child, Alice, now she did the same for Carew, despite the fact that the sight of his dark yet merry face would recall Robert so poignantly that she was hard put not to weep in the children's presence. Jeanette would not allow them more than a few minutes, as she could see how their lively presence tired their mistress. When they had gone, the room was once again quiet and butterflies would drift in the open windows on the summer breeze and flutter frantically in the tapestries. Margaret would watch their endeavours with pity and think of Elizabeth, then the tears would come and, the children gone, she would no longer make the effort to hold them back.

Kit's presence was a great consolation and he came as often as he could to sit quietly at the bedside, his eyes sometimes blue, or green or grey fixed upon hers in a tender interlocking of glances. Words were not necessary and they would hear all the sounds of High Coombe. Servants' voices calling to each other as they went about their tasks, the soft Devonian burr providing a restful bass to the harsher sounds of farm carts creaking up the drive laden with hay, the occasional snort of some great horse, as it laboured to bring in a bumper harvest on a hot afternoon. The bees and flies were humming across the garden and Margaret could see the swifts dart and swoop as they hunted the myriad insects. For Margaret and her son they were the sweetest sounds in the world. So although Kit was often away on the business which crowded in on him at Topsham and Exeter, he would return thankfully to his home. For High Coombe would always be the centre of his life, despite the fact that he had taken over Robert's great house at Rockbeare and some of the most discreet servants from London had been transferred there. He was loath to reward loyal service with dismissal, but he wanted to keep gossip about the deaths of Robert and Elizabeth to a minimum. It was inevitable that people talked and Tom Gray was sadly missed, especially at High Coombe where he had proved a firm but kindly master in Margaret's absence. Speculation was rife because everyone knew how devoted he had been to Carew as well as to Margaret and his friends could not understand why he kept away.

Kit knew that he must visit Tom's mother, his Aunt Felicity, but he put it off, pleading pressure of business to himself, but he knew that it was because he dreaded the questions, knowing her for a shrewd woman. Therefore he was horrified, if not surprised, when on an August morning just as he was about to leave his mother, an apparition rode on to the terrace at High Coombe, demanding entrance. Increasingly over the years, Felicity's appearance had emphasised her eccentricity. Even on this hot summer's day she wore voluminous skirts and a massive cloak of undyed handspun woollen cloth. The clothes seemed to be hiding the tiny creature underneath, for Felicity seemed to diminish in stature with the years. Her thick hair was now completely white and was always tangled, often with burrs, leaves, thorns or flower petals, depending on the season, and it contrasted strangely with a tanned face, dark as any gypsy's, a face curiously unlined and from which looked out piercing dark green eyes. On this particular morning, she leapt from her ambling pony and rounded on the two children, who were playing ball on the terrace under Jeanette's eye. She advanced upon them, fixing them with a terrifying glare. Bold and courageous as they were, the little creatures cowered and were relieved when their wolf-hounds began to bark. It was this sound which caught Kit's attention, for his dogs were trained to silence in these days of Margaret's sickness. The servants, who too would go about their business as quietly as they could, were alarmed by the clamour and came running from the back of the house and round the corner from the stable-yards. Felicity seemed to be cornering the two frightened children in the angle of the front bay windows and she was commanding the hounds back as well. The servants noted that although the dogs bared their teeth, they too were retreating on their bellies back against the wall. 'That one. She's a witch,' said the little nursery-maid who assisted Jeanette. Indeed that seemed to be the unanimous opinion of the servants, who stood gawping as the tiny figure rounded on them. 'Where's my Tom?' she shouted. 'Tell me that. You'm all been back weeks and I've seen no sight or sound of him.' Kit pushed his way through the muttering crowd, who gave way as they became aware of his presence.

'Come inside, Aunt,' he said quietly, 'we must talk.'

Then to his horror, she rounded again on the children, who had begun to resume their play; she said softly so that only a few servants caught her words, 'You are doomed, you know, doomed.'

Now Kit grabbed her by the shoulder and drew her inside. Unfortunately she raised her voice and it reverberated round the Great Hall which was stripped of winter hangings. 'Where is he?' she shouted. 'Where is he? I've heard that he is dead, alongside Robert Fursdon.'

Desperately Kit tried to get her into the adjoining parlour, conscious that his mother could hear all that was going on, but Felicity resisted his efforts. The curious servants were close by and heard her say, 'I've got the sight, you know. Dark deeds have been done for sure.'

Kit winced. 'Felicity, I am aware that there is gossip. But Tom is not dead. We believe that he has gone overseas.'

'That is the truth,' said a quiet voice from the gallery. Margaret, white-faced and emaciated, her grey hair hanging in lifeless strands down her back, crawled, bent over with pain, to cling to the newel post at the head of the stairs. 'I loved your son, and I would tell you if he was gone.'

Despite Kit's efforts to bar the way, Felicity began to advance menacingly towards his mother. Once again those cold sea-green eyes fixed themselves upon a victim, but this time it was Margaret. 'Penhale heiress, you who had it all, you are the one who has brought them all low, first Nicholas, dead in his prime, then Robert, your own daughter and my Tom. A loyal servant all his life, ready to do whatever was asked, to cloak your family secrets. What have you done with him?'

Kit held the old woman now, pleading with her. At the same time he called for Luke. Obviously the servants were all listening, as Luke quickly came forward. 'Take your mistress to her bed.' Luke flattened himself against the wall to escape the bony hands of the old crone as he tried to mount the stairs.

'Stop,' she cried. 'Stop. I have something to say to your mistress.' The servants behind the doors shivered. A silence seemed to fall over the whole house except where, against the great window, a chaffinch banged its wings, seeking entry. Now the old woman's voice was resonant and determined. 'I curse all Fursdons unto the third and fourth generation and I do mean those named and unnamed.' Kit prayed that the servants did not understand the reference to Carew. Kit had suffered enough, seeing his mother half-fainting, her face full of horror, and about to topple down the stairs. It was Kit who ran to catch her and carry her back to her room. It was Luke who recovered himself sufficiently to pull the old woman out of the door and back on to the terrace; fortunately the sensible Jeanette had removed the children into the garden. They would remember the witch and tell each other tales in the years to come, but they had not heard her terrible words. Now she was muttering and cursing; it took all Luke's courage to get her back on her horse and send her packing up the lane.

Felicity was more than half-crazed. Jealousy had bitten deep into her, for she had heard of Margaret's marriage to Robert with incredulity. Like Elizabeth, she regarded Margaret as singularly unattractive and she had wondered at her capacity to catch her former lover. Felicity had learnt the truth about Carew. Tom had visited her on his return from The Netherlands. His mother was laughing. 'So the love philtre worked.'

'Love philtre?' he queried.

'Yes. Your lady visited me before you carried her off. She was anxious to catch you, my lad. But then, she was with child.'

Tom paled. 'So you saw her in early pregnancy.'

'I wondered that you betrayed your other mistress.' And Felicity sneered, always jealous of Margaret's hold over her son.

Without thinking, Tom retorted, 'I did not.'

Slyly, Felicity looked at him from under hooded lids. These impulsive words gave her much food for thought in the months ahead. Tom continued to visit her and he was obviously not happy. Rumours flew about Elizabeth's flirtations. One day Felicity was visiting High Coombe with a simple for a sick cow, for she was often called upon to heal animals as well as fellow humans. Into the stable trotted a very small boy. At first Felicity thought that he was Margaret's child and that she had heard wrongly that her rival had failed to give birth to a male heir. Knowing Robert well, she saw immediately that the boy was his offspring, then she heard Jeanette call 'Carew' and she realised that he was Elizabeth's son. Rage filled her that her own son had been cuckolded and it remained even after she had confronted Tom and he had assured her that it was none of her business what he did. It was obvious to her that Tom knew about Elizabeth and Robert when he married. Why was Tom always the servant, at the beck and call of the Penhales, the Trenows and the Fursdons? Felicity brooded overlong, her mind already turned by the coven and by years of isolation and loneliness. Then Tom disappeared and she took her revenge.

The villagers had feared her for a long time. Her extraordinary career seemed to indicate a magic power to change herself, from plain country housewife to seductive lady to old crone. Now the story of the curse and her admission that she had the sight spread through the countryside. People who had consulted her for healing herbs and for love philtres now muttered under their breath about the Devil and his familiars, for Franscombe farmyard was infested with cats of all sizes and descriptions.

It was the faithful Luke who provided the spark. He had seen the whole scene at High Coombe and had witnessed his mistress's suffering which followed. Margaret did not need to be told that the tragedy was her fault; she was already eaten up with guilt. Now came the terrible fear that the curse would hold. Luke could not forgive the evil old woman for what she had done. Nor could he or Kit sleep soundly whilst they thought she carried the family's dark secrets with her. They lived in constant dread that the truth about Robert's murder and Carew's parentage would become common knowledge. On a visit to the local pot-house Luke let drop the idea that the witch's curse was upon the whole countryside. It happened that a few people were ill with the fever, and that a cow calved a monster with two heads. Then came one of those lightning summer storms when darkness came in mid-afternoon and the heavens reverberated with loud thunder-claps. Even as the storm retreated over the hill an dusk began to fall, the villagers gathered together, muttering about witches and the Devil. 'We shall never be free while she lives,' they said. More and more began to gather and to make their way towards Franscombe. They ran into the farmyard seeking out Felicity. It was her misfortune that she had caught a chill on that fateful last visit to High Coombe and she sat, feverish and exhausted, over the great fire in her kitchen. Her neighbours dragged her out by the hair. She protested in vain; the noise was overwhelming. Men, women and children were caught up in a hysterical spiral. Drown the witch and her familiars! The cats were caught by the scruff, hissing and scratching, eyes darting like fire sparks, reinforcing the conviction that they were in league with their mistress. The farm pond was full after the recent heavy rain, but thick with weed, heavy-bottomed in mud. Felicity let out a high piercing scream as they tied her hands together and cruelly drew up her legs behind. Mercifully she fainted and three burly men, laughing now that she was overcome, tossed her into the middle of the pond. Her heavy woollen garments kept her afloat so the villagers threw bricks and stones until her body sank, leaving her white face, hideous in its terror, looking up at them. A faint moon was rising behind the dark stormclouds. The more superstitious crossed themselves. The body suddenly turned over: the crowd let out a communal sigh. The children began to cry. Felicity's body sank, rose. Another sigh escaped from the group, who were beginning to retreat. The body finally sank beneath the weeds. Some of the younger lads had sport, tying stones round the cats' necks and throwing them in. Most people had left, shamefaced now. Soon they had all gone. Now the moon rose fully in all its summer splendour and the silent farmyard was etched in shadow. Nothing stirred.

21 Epilogue

News of the witch's drowning came to High Coombe. There was little relief, for Kit, still only twenty years of age, but looking at least thirty, shared his mother's last torturing weeks, as indeed did the rest of the household. Only the children were spared. It seemed to him as though the witch's curse had indeed taken root, for Margaret suffered horribly.

One evening, as the first leaves of autumn fell sighing to the ground and winds began to gather about High Coombe's sturdy stone walls, Margaret seemed to mend. She eased herself up on the bolster, took a very little liquid and talked quite coherently of the family and High Coombe. Kit felt able to tell her of Felicity's death, but not the manner of it.

Margaret smiled, 'I can die content, for you are safe. My beloved son, I am sorry to burden you so. Those dear young creatures upstairs are in your hands. To you I also bequeath Tom and Alice, so unworldly, so isolated from the horrors of life.' Here she sighed, but turned almost contentedly to look out of the high window at the dark night, to watch a branch tapping at the glass. The tapestries stirred. Diana's bow seemed to drop from her hand. 'I am happy to die here for I love this place so much. I commend it to you, along with the Fursdons. I know that you have forgiven me for my lifetime deceit; curiously, I am pleased that your name is Bourne. Trenows never belonged here, a restless breed.'

Kit leant over to smooth the bolster and push her hair from her eyes; so limited was her strength that she could scarcely lift her hands above her shoulders. Yet she went on dreamily, 'The Penhale Fursdons will survive. You, Kit, are their guardian but I do want you to marry, to find a quiet wife, who will care for you and bring you happiness.'

Before Margaret spoke again, Kit knew that she was thinking of the tempestuous Elizabeth and her careless treatment of her husband. It was no surprise to Kit when her foster-son's name sprang to her lips. 'Where is Tom now? Do you think that he did away with himself too?'

Kit was quick to give an honest reply. 'No. I am sure that he has gone to make a new life for himself, overseas. He understood that Carew was safe with us. Who knows? Some day he may return.'

Now Margaret's eyes filled with tears. She whispered, 'I shall never see him again. But tell him that I loved him still, despite...' Here her voice faded and she slept. Luke crept in and put his one gnarled hand over the one on the coverlet. 'Forgive me, master.' Then he bent to kiss it and sank down in a dark corner of the room. Kit could not have said why he stayed on too, sitting staring into the dying fire. With dawn's first light he started up, as he heard his mother say in a clear strong young voice, 'Nicholas. Oh, Nicholas, you are returned for me.' Then there was silence. Kit hardly dared to move; instinctively he sensed what he would find. Lighting a candle, he saw his mother's face, serene and smiling, the years wiped away. Kit knew that finally she was at peace.